THE GOOD DAUGHTER

S.A. MCEWEN

THE GOOD DAUGHTER

S.A. MCEWEN

ALSO BY THE AUTHOR

The Good Daughter

The Lost Boy

Good Girl Bad

Sister in Trouble

For Stephanie.
Fierce, brave, extraordinary.

PROLOGUE

MONDAY, March 26, 2018

The woman is well dressed, and the man is dead.

Her thousand-dollar Louboutins click on the marble floor as she makes her way out of the hotel room to the lift. She's unhurried; there's no one else on this floor, and the man made his own bed, so to speak. She has no qualms about leaving him lying in it.

In the lushly appointed bedroom, there's evidence of numerous lovers. Discarded high-quality bras and tiny g-strings in delicate lace, in varying sizes. Condom wrappers, champagne glasses, tousled bed sheets, and plenty of damp towels. It looks like an overindulgent orgy, starring the entitled git who's lying motionless on the lounge room floor.

White powder is carelessly cut on the glass coffee tabletop beside him. Bottles of champagne are half empty and going flat in various locations throughout the hotel room. The strong smell indicates at least some of it has been spilled sloppily on the luxurious carpet.

A silk tie hangs casually over a dining chair.

In the foyer, the woman glances without interest at the front desk, the security cameras, and the few people sitting in the hushed, plush interior. She walks out the three-metre revolving doors at the front of the building.

A few minutes later, she slips into a taxi. She pulls her long, black hair into a ponytail conspicuously, and looks the middle-aged driver in the eye.

She asks to be dropped off at a fancy café that she's never visited before, and pays with cash.

She doesn't give another thought to the dead man in the hotel room in Sydney's wealthy north shore. Rather, she enjoys her coffee, eggs, and smashed avocado without haste and without worry.

Then she goes home and gets on with her day.

1

FIVE MONTHS EARLIER – NOVEMBER 2017

NATALIE CURSORILY FLICKS through yesterday's mail, then dumps it on her kitchen bench.

The marble bench top gleams brightly. Morning sun streams in the large window overlooking the empty street. The small lounge area is neat and clean.

Natalie feels a pang of guilt, which she quickly pushes aside, as she does every fortnight after the cleaner has been to her apartment.

The cleaner is the one luxury she affords herself. Three hours once a fortnight. She tidies, vacuums, and mops—all tasks that Natalie is perfectly capable of doing herself. Her apartment isn't even very big. She doubts it takes Mali three hours to clean it, but she hates the power imbalance between them. She hates another woman cleaning up after her. She pays her far more than the going rate to assuage her feelings on the matter.

Mostly, Natalie hates that she can still hear her mother's voice on the topic, even though she's never confessed to her mother that she has a cleaner—and even though she is thirty-eight years old, and it's frankly none of her mother's business. But frugality was drummed into her from a very early age. If you were to look in the third drawer under her gleaming marble bench top, you'd find neatly folded pieces of baking paper and aluminium foil, the faint outlines of biscuits or scones visible on them. Natalie can easily use them ten to fifteen times before needing to tear off a clean piece.

In her savings account, you'd find enough to comfortably pay a deposit on a second house in Sydney's north shores.

No one opens those drawers, though, or looks in her savings account.

Natalie has lived alone for seventeen years. As soon as she finished her law degree, she fled the family home, the relief washing over her from the moment she was handed keys to her very own space.

That same relief floods through her every time she arrives back at her apartment after a family lunch, every second Sunday.

Now, however, she's still a week away from seeing her family, and she pushes them out of her mind.

She kicks off her heels and runs her fingers through her sweaty hair, collapsing on the couch, tilting her head back and closing her eyes.

Her thoughts drift back to the problem.

The tiny, minute, yet very large problem growing inside her.

* * *

"You were at the gallery last night."

Natalie had startled.

Her Uber had had a minor prang. While the driver had inspected the damage, taken photos, and exchanged numbers and license details with the other driver, Natalie had stood on the pavement, the sunshine beckoning to her like a magnet. She was soaking it up, her black hair getting hot under its rays, debating whether to walk the rest of the way home to fully enjoy it, when a man had exited the other car. He had waved dismissively at the driver, his phone glued to his ear, indicating his watch and that he'd walk the rest of the way.

Then he'd seen Natalie and had stopped dead.

She was dressed for work, her makeup flawless, her fitted red dress showing off every curve. Its neckline was perfection—classy, but showing just enough soft, tantalizing flesh that men always thought of sex. A simple choker of pearls stood out around her neck.

Her appointment had cancelled and she was heading home, the effort wasted.

At least, wasted until this man was left staring at her, speechless.

Natalie had cocked her head at him, watching. She had wished she had a cigarette—inexplicably, she felt like blowing a waft of smoke toward him. Not in his face. Just in his general direction. A challenge, maybe. A statement of independence, like she was a teenager playing truant from school, and what was he going to do about it?

It was such a clichéd moment. Hot man in suit notices sexy woman in dress.

Hot man stops and stares.

Except, in Natalie's line of work, this represented an opportunity rather than an inconvenience or an intrusion.

She wondered if the morning might not be wasted after all.

But then he had surprised her with the comment about the gallery.

He'd unceremoniously ended his call mid-sentence, as though the call was of no consequence whatsoever.

No consequence compared to her.

He fastened his dark eyes on her, and something inside her chest leapt erratically. Flashing danger signs glinted in his black eyes. For once, Natalie felt like the prey rather than the lioness.

He had stopped right in front of her, his broad shoulders and narrow hips clearly defined under his well-cut shirt. Not taking his eyes off her, he held out his hand. "Griffin," he said.

Natalie had taken his hand on automatic pilot. She felt mesmerized by his eyes. They were so dark. Framed with long, black lashes and beautiful pale skin, he looked half playboy, half wolf.

She shook his hand for a while before his half-raised eyebrow reminded her to speak. For some reason, she told him: "Ivy."

He kept hold of her hand. Emboldened by the effect he was obviously having on her, he kept it firmly in his, his thumb lightly running over her skin, his stare intense. He was thoroughly at ease in his own skin.

"You were staring at Jack Charles like you might somehow morph into him. You looked ethereal," he told her.

And somehow, all her rules had been broken.

Partly it might have been because you got the sense that people didn't say no to Griffin. Or maybe it was because he had noticed her at the art gallery—really noticed her. Not her curves, or her cheekbones, or her bewitching eyes. But her very being, in that moment, with that picture. Which had spoken to her in ways that squeezed her heart, and bruised it.

So she didn't quote him her rates. She didn't ask how long he'd like. She didn't play it for the cash. She let him take her to a hotel, and undress her, and command her, and marvel at her. She let him go down on her until she came. Really came, in the unhurried way that you can when there's no clock ticking, and the man between your legs acts like there's no place in the world he'd rather be.

She never had casual sex.

She never let herself get lost in the moment.

She never spoke to someone in the bedroom freely—unedited, unmasked.

She rarely spoke to anyone freely at all.

But Griffin was so intense, so attractive, so enamored by every inch of her, and had such presence, that she'd forgotten all the rules.

* * *

And now she was fucking pregnant. After twenty years of sexual activity so careful and pragmatic she hadn't had so much as a single itch that made her wonder if she needed an extra check up—one moment of unthinking passion, of using someone else's condom (*God, it must have broken. How old had it been? She had never had a breakage, in all her years of considerable sexual activity*), and all of that was out the window.

Then again, she doubted Griffin ever waited very long between conquests. It felt almost like a sign.

Despite this, she knew what needed to be done. She was not in any place to be a mother, even if she wanted children.

Which she didn't.

But somehow, Jack Charles's beautiful face, his story, Griffin's white-hot, insatiable desire, and her reasons for not wanting children were all tied up in a messy great ball that Natalie was in no mood to try to untangle.

She's interrupted by her mobile ringing, anyway.

"Can you come by a bit early on Sunday, Natalie?" Upeksha asks when Natalie answers the phone.

Natalie is used to the lack of preamble and pleasantries. It suits her well to get straight to the point.

For a while she had tried ignoring her mother's calls between Sunday lunches, feeling that the fortnightly interaction was quite enough family time. That only lasted until Upeksha sent a police car around to her apartment for a welfare check. The officer had peered around Natalie's door curiously.

"Your mother says you haven't answered the phone for two days." He left the statement hanging there.

Natalie had shrugged helplessly. "She fled civil war. She's always assuming the worst."

For some reason, when someone else raised their eyebrows judgementally at her mother's behavior—no matter how objectively crazy it might seem—Natalie's first impulse was violence. When it was just Natalie, deliberately letting the twelfth call go through to voicemail, her irritation and incredulity were unmatched by anyone. But the officer's slight sneer down his nose at her, his look of disbelief at the sparkling wedge of home he could see behind her, made her dig her fingernails into her palms so hard the resulting little half-moon indents in her skin could be seen for the next half an hour.

It was more than a desire to protect Upeksha. It was like a reverse mother's instinct, exacerbated; like a rabid dog. *Natalie* might be allowed to think Upeksha was completely bonkers. But this twenty-something white guy—who knew nothing of war and survival and assimilation—was most certainly not.

"Mmm," she answers her mother now, noncommittal. "What's up?"

"Your father has decided that you do so well on the stock market, that he'd like a lesson. We have some savings he'd like to trade with."

Inwardly, Natalie groans.

Her father will never trade a dollar on the stock market. Once she has shown him, in detail, how it works, he will at first think he is missing something. When it finally dawns on him the amount of risk involved, he will change his mind quick smart.

But it's no good trying to explain that to him; it's not fathomable to him that Natalie would risk her money in that way. If learning to trade is going to baffle him, learning how reckless his only daughter is with her money will baffle him even more.

Natalie agrees to help, though. Before Sunday rolls around, she'll have to come up with a way to avoid that particular lesson. Not least because she hasn't traded on the stock market for a good eight years.

Ironically, after getting her first big break from her first bad trade, she had bought her modest apartment in Sydney's middle-class South Coogee, and then had no cash left to trade with.

The lucky stock was one of her earliest purchases, before she had really learnt what she was doing. It immediately started heading downhill, and she had stubbornly refused to sell it at her stop loss, the idea of losing three-thousand dollars intolerable to her bank balance and her ego. Within a week it was at a quarter of its value. Fifteen-thousand dollars down, Natalie had never not honored a stop loss again.

But it was worth so little by then that she had forgotten about it for three years. Initially, she checked it hopefully every day, and it continued to bounce between two and four cents, a sad little line on her charts that was a painful reminder of her mistake. Her ego.

But then, routinely forgotten, her twenty-grand investment was "suddenly" worth three-hundred-thousand dollars, and Natalie was rich, by most people's standards.

Except it wasn't an investment. Natalie exclusively traded short-term, keeping stocks for less than thirty days, taking advantage of small fluctuations in the market, making only a few hundred dollars on every trade. But her three-year "mistake stock" had earned her the most money she had ever made in her entire life.

It was hard to keep remembering it was a mistake after that.

Natalie imagines her father's face. They'd sit down at the computer, his spectacles pushed to the rim of his nose, his legal pad and pen at the ready, a calculator by his elbow. He would expect Natalie to go through the process, and he'd take notes meticulously, expecting to be able to follow an A, B, C in a neat linear fashion—from the lesson to steady income once they had finished.

Ravi approached everything in life with due diligence. He combated whatever he had endured in Sri Lanka with order, patience, and as much Englishness as he could muster. Both her parents already spoke perfect English when they arrived in Australia—Ceylon being a British colony before regaining independence. But they had bought land in the whitest suburb in Sydney that they could afford. They had given their children the most Australian names they could come by. And they considered themselves as white as the next person.

Ravi would approach a lesson on the stock market in the

same way. Learn the rules, play by them. At some point, he would carefully click the lid back onto his pen, and look at Natalie in a meaningful manner. He was an incredibly smart man. He would appreciate the complexities. But he would not appreciate his daughter taking such risks with her livelihood, day in, day out.

Risk and uncertainty were not part of Ravi and Upeksha's way.

Risk could lead to standing out from the crowd.

Drawing attention to yourself.

Being different.

It could lead to surprises and uncertain outcomes.

Not that Ravi would say anything. He would look at Natalie meaningfully and expect her to step back into line.

To be sensible. To contribute. To be valuable.

To not *risk* things.

Natalie needs to find a good way to dissuade Ravi about the merits of the stock market without going through that exhausting process.

She supposes she could tell him that she no longer trades—but her current profession is hardly going to be an improvement, in his eyes.

Eventually, she settles on telling him that due to the uncertainty around the Trump presidency, she feels the stock market is too volatile at the moment. She's gone back to law.

By the time she's solved this problem, she slumps on the couch, defeated.

She doesn't make an appointment to see her doctor.

2

THE MAN WATCHES the woman carefully.

He knows her name, her height, her eye color.

He knows where she catches the bus into the city and where she frequently sees her clients.

He doesn't know what she sounds like when she laughs, or what type of wine she likes, or what she plans to be when she quits escorting in a few years' time.

He doesn't know about the homework club she volunteers at once a week to support teenagers with their learning—on the surface, or with their sense of belonging—a deeper, and more important goal.

He does know what she'll look like with his hands around her throat, though.

He's seen how that looks several times before.

3

By the time Sunday lunch rolls around, Natalie still has not made an appointment to see her doctor.

She feels decidedly queasy as she drives the thirty minutes to her parent's house in Linfield—the same house that she grew up in, that houses all her childhood memories. Occasionally, one jumps out at her, wraps her in its thick, tight, suffocating grasp—but mostly, she tries her damnedest to keep them in the past, where they belong.

Alex opens the door for her, his smile wide.

"Natty!" he cackles excitedly, reaching forward to hug her, his delight infectious. "I've missed you! I've missed you! What has kept you gone so long!" It isn't a question, more a statement of his excitement that she's here now. The conversation goes much the same way every second Sunday.

"Come," he beckons her, already heading toward the stairs leading up from the foyer to the bedrooms.

A place, Natalie knows, where it's harder to keep bad memories at bay.

"Let me say hi to Mum and Dad," Natalie says gently, nodding at him encouragingly, but a dark cloud passes across his face.

"Now! Now! Now!" he repeats, jabbing his finger toward the top of the stairs, the volume increasing with each word and each jab. Natalie sighs, and acquiesces.

His bedroom looks much the same as when Natalie left home, though he's two years older than her. Figurines of various superheroes are littered across the bed and floor. The bookshelves are lined with comic books and adventure stories. Terry Pratchett simpers from a poster above the bed.

Generally, Natalie's parents don't like her to go into Alex's bedroom without one of them present, but she has never felt afraid of her brother. He seems as manipulable as a child.

"New—see?" he says, pointing at a figurine that Natalie doesn't recognize. It stands about twenty centimeters high and has the bright, waxy look of something not yet well-handled, not worn down by hours of attention from small, grubby hands.

Except Alex's hands are not small. At six feet, he towers over Natalie, the disparity between his body and his mind as painful to her now as it is every time.

"Lovely, Alex," she tells him softly. "Tell me about him."

Alex bounces on the balls of his feet happily, recounting something about Wolverine's powers. Natalie nods encouragingly, keeping eye contact, wistfully grateful that she is able to provide this small slice of comfort in his day. His little sister—interested, warm, attentive.

He's joyful about the smallest things.

Every time Natalie sees him, her heart breaks in two all over again.

* * *

Upeksha has made enough roast to feed twelve people.

The four of them sit around the formal dining table, Alex being reminded constantly to stay at the table until he has finished his meal and excused himself.

They make stilted small talk. As always, Natalie asks after Aunty She and Uncle Pu in Melbourne, her cousins dotted around Australia. Her mother gives tight-lipped replies.

Natalie keeps in touch with these extended family members herself, of course. She doesn't know why she provokes her mother so. It's almost like she's trying to demonstrate family solidarity, draw her mother back to her heritage, her country of origin, despite knowing perfectly well that Upeksha wants nothing less. Her sister and her family epitomize all the things that Upeksha and Ravi disavowed when they fled to Australia; they celebrate their skin color. They are at home in it. They visit Sri Lanka; cook curried mutton, pickle their own fruits, and make coconut relish.

The very opposite of assimilating.

But Natalie can't let it go. She couldn't let it go twenty years ago, and she can't let it go now.

"I went to the gallery to see the Archibald exhibition a few weeks ago," she tells her family. Jack Charles is still haunting her. The portrait of the Aboriginal actor and elder by Anh Do went on to win the People's Choice Award, and Natalie can't reconcile that with the people that she experiences in her life. That they would vote for a portrait of an Aboriginal man. A stolen man. An addict. *Which people voted for his portrait?* she wonders. Submitted by a Vietnamese-born artist, no less. A refugee, surviving five days in a leaky fishing boat, attacked by two different bands of pirates on his way here.

He'd be left to rot on Manus Island if he tried to come now, Natalie thinks to herself. The thought is unbelievable, unbearable. All the things Do has contributed. What things might those languishing on Manus Island have contributed, if they'd been given a chance?

Perhaps the artistic community are different, though, Natalie thinks. *Perhaps people who care about art are slightly more evolved, more refined, carry a softness or a sensitivity that is missing on the streets.* A whole other world to the people that Natalie encounters every day. The ones who slow their cars to shout obscenities to her out the window. The ones who watch her extra carefully in David Jones.

"I liked the portrait of Jack Charles. Did you see it won the People's Choice Award?"

Natalie knows that her parents would know this. Part of being white is keeping up with the culture. Art. Literature. They would have seen Jack's face. They would have passed over it hurriedly. Moved on to more European-inspired images. Traditional.

White.

"We preferred the one of Eileene Kramer," Upeksha says, without missing a beat. "So much beauty. So much stillness. And my, what an accomplished woman at 101! Imagine that. Still working. Still travelling. Still following her passions. Can you imagine being so immersed in something that you love, that you just never retire? I guess it's like football stars. They go on to coach, to be involved in the club in other ways..."

Natalie lets the words drift over her. She knows this dance well enough by now. Her mother beats back Natalie's mutiny by sheer volume of words. She drowns Natalie in them, suffocates her subtle rebellion in a tedious snowball of white words. The football, the cricket, the current issues of being Australian. After all these years, Natalie still feels a pang of heartache at the zeal with which her mother took on anything that she considered a commitment to their new life in Australia.

Usually, it was concurrently a nail in the coffin of anything to do with Sri Lanka.

It's always this way with her family.

A constant push-pull of longing for connection to her heritage—and her parents—and finding none. Natalie longs to hear stories of where they came from, even now. Even after thirty-odd years of being deflected or outright ignored. She wants to hear the good ones and the happy ones and even the hard ones.

Especially the hard ones, perhaps. The ones that will make her weep, and despair, and fold into herself.

Her longing to know every little piece of who her parents were and what Sri Lanka was like for them is like an obsession.

To her parents, it is inconvenient at best and blasphemous at worst.

"It's not relevant," they say. "It's not important. Let's be grateful for what we have here," they tell her.

Deflect, deflect, ignore.

By the time they've had a cup of tea, Natalie is exhausted.

Alex is long gone, and she can hear him banging and shouting upstairs, his figurines fighting over imagined injustices, saving the day.

Where were they for you? Natalie thinks to herself. *Where were your heroes that day?*

She knows the answer though. They were busy pretending none of it was happening.

They were busy pretending to be white.

* * *

It's after 11 p.m. when she gets home.

She's already discarded her wig, her scalp warm and itchy from the extra layer and the weight of the thing. But her short, aggressive style didn't only horrify her mother.

To be fair, Upeksha had done everything she could to raise Natalie in a way to facilitate her fitting in. To help her to be invisible, or at least, only visible in the right ways.

Feminine ways.

Soft ways.

Ways that didn't make any trouble.

She thought that she was doing the right thing by Natalie.

But Natalie was none of those things. She was opinionated. With rough edges and strong features. She did not fade into the background. She wore her brownness like a talisman, as though in it she might belong, though the true meaning of the word was stifled underneath the way her parents attempted that very thing. Because fitting in for them meant safety and acceptance—life, even.

Natalie understood that. But she wished more than anything she could understand it in her bones. Know her parents' stories, feel them in her skin, have them as protection, as armor. Stories of survival, or heartbreak, or terror, or tragedy. Something she could belong to, whatever it was.

Because what her mother failed to understand was that being brown *did* make her different. Not to everyone. But to the kids at school who turned their noses up at her; to the parents who pulled their children away from her on the bus; to the grown men who shouted insults from their cars—Natalie *was* brown. And they rejected her.

So growing up, Natalie had found she did not belong anywhere. To her parents, the only acceptable daughter—the only *loveable* daughter—was one who was following their lead and living white. And to the white people she encountered in the schoolyard, on the bus—it didn't matter how hard she tried. She would never be white.

She was brown, and they made sure she didn't forget it.

Still, she thinks to herself now, perhaps she would grow her hair again. Though she loves it short—she feels more herself than she ever has—she hates the wig. And her bookings—and thus her income—dropped dramatically along with her long locks.

Yes, she thinks to herself. She'll grow it again, just while she's escorting. When she quits, she can always cut it off again.

She's just flicking through Netflix for something trashy and light to entertain her for half an hour when her phone pings.

Unknown: Ivy. I need to see you. Be ready tomorrow at 11. I'll pick you up. What's your address?

Natalie stares at the message, bewildered for a moment. Her work name on her private number. It makes no sense.

Then she remembers giving Griffin her number as he left. She didn't actually expect him to call, and rattled it off without much thought.

She gazes at her phone vacantly for a while.

As it happens, she has a booking tomorrow at 11 a.m. That aside, she doesn't like being told what to do.

And besides which—her line of work doesn't really lend itself to satisfying relationships. At least, that's what she tells herself as she deletes Griffin's message.

Then she books an appointment with her GP online.

4

```
James: Will you have your period? I'd
really like you to sit on my stomach
while you're bleeding.
```

NATALIE ROLLS HER EYES.

She likes her job—she really does. But men are so peculiar.

She's been emailing James for a few days, planning their date. He's been polite and respectful—anything less and she terminates the contact. At eight-hundred dollars an hour, she can afford to pick and choose her clientele.

And now, just before their meeting, this text.

What does he think, it's like a stream on command? Natalie thinks to herself. *And surely it's a little late in the planning to mention he wants something that only occurs for four days a bloody month.*

The corners of her mouth twitch at the unintended pun.

```
Natalie: No, darling, not this time.
Maybe we can plan for that next time? x

James: I'm only in Sydney for four days.
```

```
Maybe I can fly you to Brisbane at the
right time?
```

Actually, Natalie is thinking to herself that any time at the moment would probably be suitable.

She's been bleeding intermittently. She feels vaguely unwell. And for the first time in years, she is constantly thinking that there's nothing she'd like to do less than have sex.

Much to her surprise, she couldn't walk into her GP, request a termination, and have it over and done with the same day. She was utterly baffled to find out that abortion is a crime for women and doctors in New South Wales.

"But...it's 2017," was all she could think of to say, staring at the doctor in disbelief.

The doctor had shrugged, surprised that Natalie was unaware of this. "I need to ascertain that a termination is necessary to protect your mental or physical health. It's relatively easy to show. But you'll need to expand on your reasoning a little for me."

It seemed completely ludicrous that she could not just state "I don't want children" and proceed accordingly. It was her body, after all. Natalie had never thought much about women's rights or feminism, because she felt like she was afforded far more freedom and respect as a woman than she was as a colored person, and her ponderings on privilege were always focused on race. But at this point in her life—pregnant, nauseous, and slightly shocked to find herself in this predicament—Natalie felt the stirrings of rage.

It wasn't like she hadn't felt rage before. But this felt like a different kind of rage. A less quiet rage, that she could take home and rationalize away, talk herself down into a space where she could go back into the world without it.

This felt like a more violent kind of rage.

Because what could she tell the doctor that would convey the terror and pain and panic that swirled around in her at the thought of having children? How could she explain Ravi and Upeksha and Alex in a way that any upper-middle-class white doctor would understand? The disconnect she felt from them, from herself, from everyone? God, she was barely able to nurture herself. A child was out of the question.

This ends here, was what she would have said, if only she could adequately convey the past thirty-eight years to her doctor in that phrase, in her six-minute appointment.

But it was hard to pin down, let alone convey. How do you communicate the scope of how petrified Natalie was of parenting? The sheer enormity of it. Of passing it on. This inability to *feel* things. To connect with other people on a deeper level. Her parents had, after all, only tried to make her and Alex feel safe. How they had succeeded only in making the world seem terrifying was unclear to Natalie. All she knew, deep in her bones, was that she did not feel whole enough herself to do any better. Both she and these unborn, imagined children would be far, far better off if they never actually met.

But family and children were the *point,* to most people that Natalie knew. They were joy and connection and love and *life.*

So Natalie just muttered that she was not with the father, and was not in an emotional position to raise a child on her own.

She had taken the pamphlets and phone numbers provided and walked home in an enraged, confused daze.

* * *

Now, two weeks after that appointment, Natalie puts her phone and James's bizarre requests away, and turns back to Eloise.

"I can't bloody work for two weeks afterwards. I had to wait until there were some bookings I could shift," she says, referring to the termination she has delayed until the following day.

Eloise is not impressed.

"Surely this takes priority over men's libidos? Christ, Nat, especially if you were feeling sick. How did you work through that?"

Natalie shrugs.

"Sex work is all about putting on a show of sorts, no matter what you feel like. It really wasn't that hard."

They're sitting at a trendy Sydney café, enjoying brunch in the sunshine. Natalie is painfully conscious of her mother's likely response at family lunch later in the day. The tight lips, the frown when Natalie doesn't eat three servings. Even tighter lips when she makes her excuse about brunch with Eloise.

But you knew you had family lunch, Upeksha would be thinking. *Why would you go out for brunch just before lunch with the family?*

Natalie and Eloise have been friends since law school. Eloise is a high-flying human rights lawyer. She even looks a bit like Amal—tall, dark, striking. Feminine. She's unphased by Natalie's defection to sex work, and one of only two friends who are aware of it.

She's more interested in the pregnancy than the client requesting menstrual blood splatter, however.

"How are you feeling about the termination?"

Natalie hesitates. She doesn't really know how to answer that, and her stomach tightens at the thought. But she feigns a confidence that she doesn't feel.

"Indifferent. It doesn't even feel like a termination. It's just medication. Then bleeding and cramps, apparently."

It's not that she can't be honest with her friend. It's more that she's not being entirely honest with herself, though Natalie doesn't recognize that, even as she hesitates.

"Surely in your line of work you should be on the pill, not relying on condoms?"

Natalie shrugs and shakes her head. "I don't like the pill. It makes me feel crazy. Angry. Something. Also, I've never had a condom break before. Ever. And, ironically, it wasn't even with a client. It was some hot guy who accosted me on the street."

Eloise drops her fork back on to her plate with a clatter. She looks shocked. She can't remember the last time Natalie had sex just for fun.

"Don't you usually just give them your card?" she murmurs, trying to recover a neutral face.

"I thought about it. But I wanted to have sex with him. So I went with the flow. He keeps texting me, actually."

Eloise's fork, which she'd just picked up, is placed gently down again. "And?" she asks nonchalantly, almost as though worried that if she looks too enthusiastic, she'll scare Natalie off the topic.

"I was all done up for work. I had a cancellation. So really, he met Ivy. I even told him my name was Ivy," Natalie shrugs again. "So it was just a lovely aberration, really. You know how I feel about relationships while working."

Eloise looks at Natalie shrewdly. "I know how you feel about *relationships*," she returns. Her concern about Natalie's ability to shut people out existed long before sex work was used as a justification. "Sometimes, I think you chose this work so you have an excuse not to have a go at being close to someone."

"I chose this work to pay for Alex's medical expenses," Natalie says, terse, though that is not strictly true, either. Working as a lawyer would have more than covered any gaps. Not even Natalie is sure why she said that. She's never felt the need to justify her choice before. She chose sex work because she wanted to do it.

"Also, it suits me," she adds. "I was too lazy to deal with working til 8 p.m. every night. I don't know how you can still function at that time. Law is the crazy job if you ask me, not sex work."

* * *

Afterwards, on the drive to her parents' place, Natalie tries to pin down how she feels about the termination.

The truth is, she feels worse about it than she can articulate.

She imagines holding a baby in her arms, and her stomach flip-flops all over the place.

It's not longing of any sort. She has never been maternal. She has never ooh-ed and ahh-ed over other people's babies. She's looked at them with slight distaste, their shrivelled little old-man faces, their screams. Their mess.

So it's not longing.

It's more a sort of questioning. Second-guessing herself.

She's not superstitious either, but nevertheless, it feels like some kind of sign.

The one time she has sex for pleasure, not cash.

The one time the condom breaks—at least, as far as she knows.

The one time a man keeps infiltrating her thoughts.

Griffin has texted twice more. The perfect texts. Not needy. Not pleading. Not disgruntled that she hasn't replied. Just persistent. Upping the flirtiness, when she didn't respond to the bossier one, and completely at ease with himself. Unafraid to convey that he wants her.

All the things she has never wanted are all converging, right now, being handed to her on a silver platter.

The man.

The hot, perceptive, sex-god man.

The baby.

She's thirty-eight. It's now or never.

A normal life.

Natalie shakes her head. Where are these thoughts coming from? Is it just fear of missing out? That once that window closes, it's closed for good? The ticking clock? *Do all women who haven't wanted children their whole lives have this moment of doubt?* she wonders to herself.

For someone who thinks she knows her own mind remarkably well, this uncertainty and second-guessing is unnerving. Unsettling. She needs to think.

Thinking, of course, is difficult at her parents' house.

Natalie walks up to the front door slowly.

Alex greets her as he always does.

Natalie feels the tightness in her chest as she always does.

Despite her brunch, she does her best to eat copiously.

Upeksha nods in satisfaction.

5

NATALIE IS SUPPOSED to be thinking about sex.

Sex with Marek, in particular.

But she's not. She's thinking about race. Again.

Her mother would be mortified. Firstly that Natalie was on all fours, being gently lathered in soap and then patted dry by an older man—a brown one, no less. Secondly that she was in this position for money—though the amount of money in question would give her pause. Escorting Natalie-style is not the seedy type of affair you see referenced in popular sitcoms.

In particular, though, Upeksha would be mortified that Natalie was once again thinking about race. Because, if it were not for the fact that Marek was brown, Natalie had just realized, she would probably consider this a racist fetish—if it were a white man, cleaning a brown woman before sex could seem sinister. And now she was not only thinking about race during work, which Marek was paying an astoundingly large amount of money for, and probably deserved more of her attention—but she was also thinking about her mother.

She pulls herself back to the present.

Marek is a new client, which is always a stressful experience.

Natalie can't let her guard down with new clients. She thinks she's a good judge of character, good at reading people—but then, there was that guy at the Radisson who seemed so gentle and attentive, and then tied her up and wouldn't untie her at the end of his booking. He'd jeered at her and called her a *sloppy black cunt* and had verbally terrorized her for twenty minutes before releasing her, refusing to pay. It was the only time she hadn't been paid in eight years of escorting. It still stung. Not the loss of money—the fact that it left their sex as something murky. Not a transaction where both parties got what they came for.

It was an abuse. An attack. An exertion of power.

God, she thinks to herself now, nearly patted dry. She is being a very lackluster guest for poor Marek.

Still. She hopes the bath over the dining table is as weird as it's going to get.

LATER, she's sitting in silence with Eloise over dinner when her phone pings.

> Griffin: Not even a coffee? Not even a pash?

Eloise snatches it up.

"I'm going to accept," she says, keying in Natalie's passcode without missing a beat.

"Don't you dare," Natalie warns, her tone mild. She knows Eloise won't actually send the message. "How do you know my passcode, anyway?"

"Darling, you've used the same passcode for every phone and bank card you've ever had for as long as I've known you. I could empty your bank accounts if I wanted to."

Natalie snatches her phone back. She looks at Griffin's message, wondering.

But then she remembers all the reasons it's a bad idea, and puts it away.

"Just go for a coffee," Eloise urges. "He sounded fun."

"He was indeed fun," Natalie says, "but fun, at some point, will turn into telling him I'm an escort. And then things will start to get un-fun very quickly."

"You don't know that. You've said lots of the escorts you know have relationships."

"They have relationships. I didn't say they were functional relationships. I don't know any of them well enough to ask. But I find it hard to imagine how you negotiate having sex with other men in your relationship, without there being so much weirdness that it blows up in your face." Personally, Natalie doesn't think it matters in the slightest. It feels like any job to her. But she feels doubtful that any old guy she picked up on the street—literally—would be evolved enough to cope with it. Most men, she suspects, would freak the fuck out.

Natalie doesn't mention to Eloise the other problem relating to Griffin, though. That, in fact, she has not yet had an abortion. That she is now beyond the time when she can have a medical abortion, and needs to have a surgical one.

It's not that she doesn't trust Eloise or value her opinion. It's more that she does not even recognize the Natalie who cancelled the appointment. She can't talk about it because she does not have any actual words to say. All she has is a feeling, an uneasiness, a sense of something bad approaching.

In her mind, she wants to say it's biology: her body fighting against her essence, her soul. The hormones, maybe, coursing through her veins, sending messages that she doesn't want to hear.

That she would never have been receptive to had that condom not broken.

Is it possible that messages are distorted once hormones start running amok in your body? she wonders. The message has been simple and clear for as long as Natalie can remember.

No children.

Why was it getting jumbled now? It's inconvenient and infuriating. Natalie can't work out what she truly thinks under all the other noise.

"Well, I have some other news," Eloise says, bringing her back to the present. "It's about Grant Boyd."

Natalie's focus switches gears seamlessly. Worries about relationships and fetuses fade into irrelevant background noise.

"He's being released from his latest stint in Long Bay. He served four years of a six-year sentence. I don't know why anyone ever lets him out. He'll be back in within the year, I guarantee it."

Natalie nods. She relies on Eloise to do the digging about this particular case, to keep her informed. They agreed that this was a way for Natalie to not get immersed in it.

Unhealthily.

"There's more, though." Eloise hesitates, concern in her eyes. Natalie just nods at her. She's heard the worst news she could ever hear regarding Grant Boyd. She is sure nothing else will ever compare.

"His parents were both killed in a car crash a couple of years ago. And for his parole he's moving back into their home."

Natalie digests this information without responding.

Grant Boyd living a few houses down from her parents is not acceptable.

But living that close to Alex is enraging.

"Nat?" Eloise asks a few moments later. Natalie becomes aware of shredding her napkin. She places it back on the table, smooths it down, and puts her hands neatly in her lap. Then she looks back up at Eloise.

"Is there anything we can do?" she asks in a low voice, though she knows the answer.

She presses her teeth together after speaking, her jaw clenching painfully, to prevent herself from grinding them.

"I've already left a message with the parole officer. I'll ask for a stipulation to be added, that he doesn't go near their house or approach any of them. That's about as much as we can do."

Natalie nods. She feels slightly breathless.

Later, impulsively—recklessly—she texts Griffin.

```
Natalie: Sure. How about coffee tomorrow
at 10?
```

His response dings through immediately.

```
Griffin: I thought you'd never ask.
```

6

He THINKS everything is going according to plan.

Trust has been established.

Now, it's just a matter of time. Time and opportunity.

This is the best one yet.

But he needs to be patient.

Everything has to be just right.

Everything has to be perfect.

So that there can be this time, and a next time, and another.

Good things come to those who wait.

He must wait for the right moment to make the next move.

7

"I WAS JUST about ready to give up on you."

Griffin is sitting across from Natalie, his eyes boring into her much like they did that first time. She feels undressed, exposed by his gaze. She squirms uncomfortably.

"I have a busy life," she says uneasily, wrapping both hands around her coffee, feeling suddenly cold, though it's a bright early summer morning, warmth and promise radiating off the pavement on her walk here.

Now that they're seated, Natalie can't quite work out why she proposed this meeting after all. Was it just an amateur attempt to shake off the bad feelings associated with Grant and abortions and her ticking clock? Sex was, after all, a distraction in itself.

She didn't turn to sex work because she hated sex.

"So do I. But I make time for the important things."

At this, Natalie just manages to stop herself from rolling her eyes. *Which part of our last encounter makes this important?* she thinks, assuming he is referring to the sex. Which was, frankly, pretty memorable—and that is saying something, for Natalie, amidst a sea of often really very interesting sex.

"It was a sign, our cars crashing," he says, not smiling. "I knew

I'd missed an opportunity at the gallery to meet you. I don't often let opportunities pass me by." Then he smiles, his eyes crinkling pleasantly, his intensity softened by the twinkle in his eyes. "So you see, it was meant to be."

Natalie shivers again. She doesn't need someone else filling her head with signs and superstition.

Still, sitting across from her in his nicely cut suit, with his black eyes and his sexy stare, Natalie can't help but respond to him. She finds his attraction to her almost embarrassing, but still she feels a throbbing between her legs. And what was she here for, after all? *A distraction,* she thinks to herself. *A distraction from all the other stuff going on in my life.*

So she relents a little.

He doesn't ask where she's from, or even about her heritage, which is a good start. He asks about her work (she lies) and what she likes to do in her spare time (she tells him painting, brunch with friends, quiet mornings with the newspaper or a good book —the truth).

He tells her about his business: importing and exporting various items that she doesn't understand and has absolutely no interest in.

He tells her that he enjoyed their encounter last month more than he has enjoyed anything in years. As he says that, he takes her hand, traces a finger along the inside of her wrist and around her palm.

"I want you," he tells her, his voice low and sexy. "Come home with me."

* * *

Home, it turns out, is Sheraton on the Park.

Now that he has her where he wants her, some of his intensity dissipates. He pours her a glass of Riesling, though it's barely midday, and agrees that this is not, in fact, his home.

"I live out of a suitcase a lot. Trips to China, Singapore, all the major Australian cities. Sometimes, I wonder whether there's any point in having a house at all."

"You've got to have somewhere to keep all your stuff," Natalie replies absentmindedly. Disinterestedly, perhaps. The room is beautifully appointed, but she's used to being in nice hotel rooms. She wonders what Griffin would say if he knew. "Where is this pointless house, anyway?"

"Melbourne," he replies, clinking his glass to hers, a neat whiskey, then patting the couch beside him. They're facing floor-to-ceiling windows overlooking the bay. "Do you get there much?"

"Sometimes, for work," Natalie replies, which is true. She regularly tours Melbourne for four or five days at a time, meeting new clients, catching up with friends. But she lets Griffin imagine it in the context of lawyer-ing.

She takes small sips of her wine. Conscious of the little life inside her. Wondering what that means. *Just in case,* she tells herself hastily.

Suddenly, seeing Griffin again seems futile. Not only has she failed to mention she is, right this minute, carrying his child, but she has told him lie after lie about her work-related activities. She curses her spontaneity in landing her here. Nothing good is going to come of this.

"Well, I should get going," she says, moving to stand up, though she has barely touched her wine and they have only been in the hotel for about seven minutes. But Griffin puts a hand on her leg, and he might as well have lain on top of her. She *wants* him to lie on top of her. Naked. Licking and touching her like he did last time. Drawing her so far out of herself, her usual role in sex, that she gets lost in the moment.

"I want to kiss you. Now," Griffin says. He's so commanding, so sure of himself. He takes complete control, and Natalie loves relinquishing it. She feels freer than she has in a long, long time.

As he leans in toward her, his hand slides ever so slightly up her thigh. It's a suggestion, a promise, a message for her rather than a touch to satiate himself. Already she longs for his hand to go higher, for his fingers to slide under her briefs, for him to feel how wet she is, to part her lips and push inside her.

To tell her what to do next.

Instead, his lips brush against hers. His other arm comes around her waist and pulls her into him firmly, one sharp, well-defined movement that is almost possessive. His kiss is soft and slow, just his lips, slightly parted, kissing her bottom lip and then her top lip. She's used to men tasting her hastily, urgently, all about their needs, their desires. Griffin is teasing her. He wants her to want him. His kisses are perfection; it is Natalie who deepens the kiss, flicking her tongue along his upper lip, parting her lips wider, inviting him in. She wants his tongue, his fingers, his touch.

His everything.

But he holds it all back, continuing to tease her, running his fingers infuriatingly close to where she wants them and then pulling them away, starting again, the hint of a smile dancing around his lips, until she is beside herself and has to take back the lead. She pushes him backward, into the couch, then straddles him, fixing him with her own sexy stare.

At last she can feel some friction against her clit. In this moment the bulge in his pants is everything she can imagine ever wanting again. She curls her fingers into his hair, pulling his head back, looking down at him hungrily before lowering her mouth back to his, kissing him deeply. Grinding against him. Relishing his tongue.

Then he's pushing her back gently. "Stand up," he commands, and Natalie obeys without hesitation.

"Turn around. Put your hands on the table."

Natalie obliges, the low coffee table leaving her arse out in front of Griffin. Slowly, he pushes up her skirt and peels down her panties. She can feel him spreading her lips, but he doesn't touch her.

Eventually, what feels like hours later, she hears him groan.

"You're so pretty down here," he murmurs. "I want to look at you and lick you and fuck you all at once."

AFTERWARDS, they go to the gallery.

The Archibald works have been replaced by 19th-century watercolors.

Natalie feels at once bereft and relieved to not see Jack Charles. She doesn't want to explain what he means to her, why she had been staring at him the way she had when Griffin first saw her. It's hard to explain to white people, without sounding whiney or angry—neither of which are welcomed, Natalie has found. It's hard for people to see it, if they just don't. And usually, alongside a companion like Griffin, the incursions are limited. People don't shout at her to *go home you black cunt* when she's with a well-dressed white man.

What can you say, by way of explanation? That just last week, waiting in line at the bank, the teller called the white woman behind her in the queue. When Natalie had said politely, "Excuse me, I think I was next," the woman had looked surprised. "Oh, I thought you two were together," she'd said, indicating the elderly brown man who was being served by another teller. At a guess, Natalie would have said his heritage was Indian, not Sri Lankan.

The teller didn't even have the self-awareness to look mortified.

Natalie had wanted to say, well surely then you would assume this white woman behind me is with that elderly white man over at that teller? But she had learnt a long time ago talking about race was almost always interpreted as aggression. She'd merely shook her head no, and approached the teller, her anger simmering lightly inside.

Would Griffin see that as racist? Natalie wonders. Assuming the only two brown people in the queue must be together. She doubts it. "Just a misunderstanding," he might say. "Harmless mistake."

Not that *racist* is a word she ever utters aloud, except to her parents, who refute its existence at every turn.

But what about the bomb squad at the airport, she could counter. *Why am I picked, every time?* "Coincidence," people have said to her, before.

Or the insults on the street? "Bad eggs," she has heard, countless times.

Natalie would like to say that these instances are so everyday that she doesn't feel them anymore. That she can shrug them off.

That there are enough good people in her life that she can ignore the "bad eggs."

But it's simply not true. They add up, all these little incursions on your dignity, your self-worth.

Maybe they add up to despair, or depression, or suicide.

Or maybe they add up to rage.

That day, looking at the portrait of Jack Charles, Natalie's mood had lent more toward confusion. It was as though she was trying to reach into something fundamental to understand it. The duplicity. The hypocrisy. That a culture could at once hold up Jack Charles—as they should, of course—but at the same time, turn a blind eye to refugees, to the poverty and racism and health gaps that plagued Aboriginal communities, to the scapegoating and fear-mongering of conservative politicians about whole races. *African gangs, for God's sake.*

To the relentless, everyday incursions that she experienced.

Griffin had thought she looked ethereal.

She had really just felt betrayed.

8

AT FAMILY LUNCH the next week, Natalie fidgets at the table, pushing her food around her plate, her stomach clenching with nerves.

"I have bad news," she says.

She's not worried about upsetting her parents.

She's worried about them upsetting her.

"Grant Boyd is being released in a few days' time. He's moving into number seven."

Ravi and Upeksha are composed. If they feel anything, they don't show it. Both look down at their food with great interest.

"He served his time. We have nothing but best wishes for that boy. Don't worry about us, Natalie."

Natalie clenches her jaw, tries not to grind her teeth. "He's been in and out of jail on assault charges his whole life. He's a racist little shit—"

Here her mother cuts her off sharply. "Natalie. Language." Her voice and her eyes are sharp. She glances at Alex meaningfully.

Natalie glances at Alex meaningfully, too.

"He's hurt you before. He might hurt you again," she says

quietly, but her shoulders slump. She's defeated already. The united front of her parents' forgiveness, their placid acceptance is more than she can bear. Certainly more than she can fight against and hope to achieve anything.

She pushes her plate away. And takes some satisfaction in it being her turn to stare at her food, her resistance to her parents' stance every bit as wilful as their resistance to hers.

9

THAT EVENING, Natalie tries to forget about her parents with a friend.

"I've deferred next year," Letitia announces, brushing crumbs off her hands to toss her long, black hair over her shoulder.

Letitia is the only sex worker who Natalie has ever invited to her apartment.

She's the only one that she really talks to, if truth be told. What started out as a mentoring type of role has evolved into a robust friendship.

Natalie stops on her way over to the couch with their drinks, midway across the room.

Letitia doesn't notice, and digs back in to the cheese laid out on the coffee table. A vase of vibrant, fresh hydrangeas glows a deep blue next to the cheese.

"Why?" Natalie asks, trying not to sound motherly and disapproving, though that is exactly what she feels. Letitia is far too young to be deciding to only escort.

"I'm having too much fun, earning too much money, and I just want to enjoy myself for a while. I would never have dreamed of visiting London before now, ever!" she declares happily, extending an arm for the fancy Riesling Natalie is not handing over. She is still standing in the middle of the room, dismayed.

"But you need a fall-back plan. This industry can change on a dime. You don't want to be left without skills or with gaps in your resume."

"It's just for a year. I want to buy a house and travel as much as I can. Then I'll settle back down and become an engineer, don't worry."

As much as she tries not to, Natalie feels protective toward the woman. They've only known each other for a year, with Letitia emailing "Ivy" to ask for some tips about starting escorting. She was struggling to manage her studies and her finances, and like many students before her, looked to the oldest profession in the world to help her along. *I was top of my class in school, and I'm loving engineering,* she had written, *and it seems ridiculous that STILL, the most money I can earn is from my body. But why the hell not? I like sex, and I feel like I could do this. I'd love to talk to you about it, if it's not too much to ask.*

It had actually been too much to ask. Natalie had turned down similar requests before, or quoted newbies a mentoring rate that soon saw them scurrying in the other direction, slinking around ebook websites for a "how-to" guide for one hundredth of the price. But Letitia had skin color on her side; Natalie felt a responsibility to help her. To guide her not just as an escort, but as an escort of color. To alert her to the differences. To make sure she was okay.

It was the most maternal she had ever felt.

"Okay, well..." Natalie sits down, takes a sip of her wine. She's come to value their catch-ups as much, if not more than Letitia, who by now knows the ropes and has settled in to sex work for the long haul. New women start all the time; most of them don't last. The work is hard, and it's not for everyone. It takes a certain type of warmth coupled with a capacity for disconnection—a difficult combination to pull off, to not be damaged by it. "Just make sure you have other skills to fall back on. Make some money, make some good investments, but have a plan to fall back on for if you get sick of it. You're too young to have your perceptions of men tainted forever."

It's not that Natalie meets bad men.

It's that she meets such ordinary ones.

Kind, respectable, thoughtful ones. Most often, married, lying, cheating ones. They're so everyday it's terrifying.

Is that why I haven't replied to Griffin again? she wonders. All that travel. He's almost certainly got an escort on speed dial in every city. She's seen it too many times to believe anyone doesn't do it. And she knows that that is unreasonable—but that's the cost of sex work, for her.

Not trusting any man.

She doesn't take on board Eloise's little insights—that perhaps this is not about men at all. That sex work might be a simple explanation that Natalie gives herself and others for avoiding intimacy, when the problem had actually existed long before sex was work in Natalie's life.

"How are your folks?" Letitia asks, and Natalie grimaces.

"The same."

"I thought they were sweet."

Letitia had dropped by with some lingerie she had borrowed for a photo shoot, at a time when Ravi and Upeksha were having a cup of tea at Natalie's. It was unusual enough that they visited her ("We haven't seen your place for years!" they'd said, wearing down her resolve to keep them at bay), but Letitia dropping in at the same time was a one in a million chance. She'd passed her off as a law student, interviewing her for a paper. At the time Natalie was supposedly trading the stock market, but if her parents noticed this, they didn't mention it.

"They are sweet. Unless you're their daughter, and acting a little too aware of your skin color."

"Fair enough," Letitia laughs, a deep, throaty laugh that vibrates the air between them. She's all woman, not a trace of self-consciousness in her. "What else is happening?"

For a moment, Natalie considers confiding in her about Grant. But she's still feeling hollow following the conversation with her parents. It's not even that they don't want to stab him a little, the way that Natalie does. It's that they're not on her team. She wants to live in a world where she belongs, regardless of her skin color. Her parents try to belong by rejecting their skin color, without seeming to care that that means rejecting her too.

Instead, Natalie tells Letitia about Griffin. Her unusual burn of desire when she looked at him. Her mistrust.

"This is what a relationship looks like as a hooker." She grins wryly. "Doubt and misgivings."

"It doesn't have to," Letitia counters. "What's the worst that could happen? Why not just give it a go?"

"There are too many ways it's likely to fail. He probably uses escorts. He probably won't like me being an escort. And besides those two doozies...I was never very good at relationships anyway. Intimacy, compromise. Erghhh." Natalie shudders with distaste.

She puts her wine down, torn, yet again, about the baby.

She has another appointment. This time for a surgical abortion.

She's eleven weeks pregnant.

* * *

Walking Letitia to the ground floor exit later, Natalie remains engrossed in their conversation.

Neither of them notice the figure hunched low in the front seat of the car across the road, dark glasses hiding cold eyes, which are staring straight at them.

They hug—a firm, tight hug with meaning. Then Letitia walks out of the automatic doors and turns toward the bus stop. Natalie watches her retreating back, her heart clenching a little.

Letitia might be the closest she has allowed anyone to get to her in a very long time.

———

10

"CAN I SEE IT?"

It's an odd request, Natalie knows. She's fasted. She's taken the drugs. She's in her surgical gown, waiting to be wheeled into theatre.

And suddenly she wants to see the little creature growing inside her.

The nurse looks at her with something close to irritation, just for a second. "Of course," she says, her tone falsely kind and concerned, a complete mismatch to the initial flash of scorn she had not managed to hide.

Natalie imagines she's thinking, *who books a termination then has second thoughts?* Then Natalie thinks she's probably just annoyed at the administrative delay it will result in—not judging her personally, not judging her choices. Because it's a big decision, right? Surely lots of people struggle with it?

She has to wait a long time. It feels like hours, but maybe it's not. Everything seems to be moving in slow motion. It's the anxiety overlaying this choice, this action.

Just say this is my only chance to have a baby?

Finally, a young, energetic doctor bounces into the room.

"You want us to check the fetus?" she asks, indicating two nurses who have followed her into the room. She grabs Natalie's chart off the end of the bed and starts skimming it. "These guys will take you to the ultrasound. I'll be along in about ten minutes; we'll have a look at how things are going."

Natalie opens her mouth to correct her, but she's already bounced back out, her competence and confidence radiating from her, her ponytail swinging.

Natalie wishes she had a friend with her to hold her hand.

* * *

When the doctor returns, warning her about the coldness of the lubrication she smears across her still-flat stomach, Natalie tries again.

"I'm booked for a termination. I just wanted to see it."

The doctor's air of confidence falters a little.

"You're having second thoughts about the procedure."

"Yes. No. I'm not sure."

She's in the private ward of the North Shore Private Hospital. It might be unusual, but the doctor recovers quickly.

"Of course. Let's have a look."

She adjusts the screen so that Natalie can see it, and presses the ultrasound wand into her stomach. At first there is nothing, and the doctor moves the wand around, pressing hard. It's uncomfortable, and Natalie grimaces.

"There!" The doctor says at last. "Listen." She turns a few knobs, and thudding fills Natalie's ears. There's something perverse about it: the loudness in the small room.

Held up so piercingly against the purpose of her visit.

In that sound, Natalie hears so much life.

"There's the head," the doctor indicates a white blob, the screen black and streaky. "And the legs." Then she starts to frown, stops talking to Natalie. For a minute or two she frowns and pushes, moving the wand this way and that. Natalie can't make out much of anything.

The *ba-boom, ba-boom, ba-boom* fills the room.

The doctor turns some more knobs and the sound disappears. She turns the monitor back toward her, so only she can see it.

"I'm sorry," she murmurs eventually, concern clouding her eyes as she looks over at Natalie. "There seem to be some abnormalities."

Natalie struggles to sit up, and the doctor places a gentle hand on her thigh, the gesture indicating she should lie back. "Let's make you comfortable, then we can talk."

"No!" Natalie responds sharply, thinking, how on earth was one supposed to get comfortable after being delivered the news that your baby was abnormal? Even if you were minutes away from terminating it. "Tell me what's wrong."

"I'm not sure exactly," the doctor responds, looking at Natalie carefully. "Some of the organs appear to have formed on the outside of the body. The heart is strong, but it is not a viable fetus. It won't survive. I'm so sorry."

Natalie nods dumbly.

It has taken the question out of her hands, the need to make the right decision. The "last chance" nature of it. The questioning.

But now she feels empty. Distressed.

Alone.

"Can I proceed with the termination, then?" she says softly to the doctor, who gently starts to talk to her about her options. If she wants to find out more about what has gone wrong.

When she gets to the part about waiting until she miscarries, in order to run tests on the tissue, Natalie holds a hand up to silence her.

The doctor nods silently and leaves the room.

Shortly, two nurses come to take her to theatre.

The anaesthetist walks by her head, talking her through what happens next, but his words are a meaningless hum in her ears.

Natalie stares at the ceiling and watches the fluorescent lights flash by.

11

When Griffin next calls her, Natalie is neck-deep in *Buffy the Vampire Slayer* DVDs and self-pity.

"I'm sick," she tells him. Her voice does indeed sound scratchy and hoarse, but this is actually from the many bouts of crying she has experienced, rather than from any virus.

The tears make no sense to Natalie. It's not like she had wanted a baby. Nevertheless, she feels bereft.

She does not feel like sex, with clients or with Griffin.

"I'll bring you some soup," he tells her, and even though she doesn't want him to see her in her flannel pyjamas with her red-rimmed eyes, she also longs for someone to come and look after her. So she tells him her address, and unlocks her door.

When he arrives, he busies himself in her kitchen, locating bowls and utensils. The smell of rich tomato-based soup fills the small apartment.

"I can't claim to have made it." He smiles at her, his proficiency in both the kitchen and the caring stirring something deep inside her. "But it's my favorite comfort food when I'm in Sydney and feel a bit lonely."

He carefully places two bowls on the coffee table, then returns with some fresh, buttered bread.

He raises his eyebrows at Buffy, frozen mid-fight on the screen, her face fierce and focused. "Shall we?" he says, indicating the remote, and Natalie's heart flutters.

It's just because I'm feeling vulnerable, she tells herself, the general anaesthetic and the diversion from her usual routine playing havoc with her mood and with her energy levels.

But she can't remember the last time she gave herself up to being nurtured by someone.

She can't remember the last time there was someone there who *wanted* to be nurturing, let alone was capable of succeeding at it.

She snuggles into Griffin, with soup and *Buffy*, and feels something dangerously close to longing. For this to be the norm, not the exception in her life. For this to result in stirring feelings of contentedness for what she has, rather than longing for what she wishes she had more of.

For a moment, she feels the overwhelming urge to tell him about the baby. *Their* baby. To share the burden, and the pain, and the confusion. Though she doesn't frame it as such, it's a desire—for once—to hand her care over to someone else, to trust that they'll look after her soft and vulnerable parts. An almost childlike request: *Can you look after this for me for a while?*

Please?

It's too big for me right now.

But she's never experienced such a thing, and she doesn't even know the words to use to ask for support, let alone have any trust that someone will hold her the way she needs to be held.

She laps up the physical comfort of Griffin. But she stays silent on the topics that might soothe her to talk about. The ones that might help her to fulfil the yearning for connection that she doesn't understand.

* * *

The next morning, Griffin has to leave early.

After spooning her all night, his body warm and solid against her, he slips out from under the bedcovers and is dressed before she even stirs.

He plants a kiss on her forehead, murmuring "Get well," and eases out of the room.

For a moment in the kitchen, he stares again at the pile of mail addressed to someone who's name is not Ivy, on the otherwise sleek and sparkling kitchen bench.

Then he quietly lets himself out.

Natalie sleeps for another few hours.

She sleeps better than she has in a long, long time.

12

CHRISTMAS COMES AND GOES, and Natalie still hasn't gone back to work.

Letitia joined her family for Christmas lunch, her own parents being in Jamaica, and it made the day surprisingly tolerable. Old and new wounds and habits were disrupted by her presence and kept at bay. Natalie avoided mentioning Grant Boyd, or even glancing at number seven as she pulled up outside her parents' house that morning. And if her parents had encountered him, they kept that to themselves.

Letitia's easy laughter rang out from the backyard all afternoon. Even the lies were easy: Letitia stating she'd switched to an engineering degree; that she was living on savings so she didn't have to work.

Alex was thrilled to have an additional guest, only making a couple of inappropriate comments. But Natalie had worded Letitia up on the impact of his brain injury long ago—the impulsiveness, the lack of inhibitions, the difficulty concentrating and remembering things—so she was neither surprised nor uncomfortable.

On the way home, Letitia had been quieter.

"Your parents are very patient," she observed softly, and Natalie had nodded.

They drove in silence for a while.

Whatever issues she has with her parents herself, Natalie knows this is true, and is grateful. She hates to imagine what would have happened to Alex without them. She tries not to think about what will happen after they pass.

It's hard to describe to other people exactly what Alex needs support with. He can present so differently, depending on the context. He holds down a permanent job, he gets himself ready for work every morning. He looks well-groomed—handsome, even.

But these things have taken so much time. So much support. Occupational therapy. Neuropsychology. Speech therapy. Even physiotherapy, for support with movement and balance. Support for the family to implement strategies.

And repetition.

So much repetition.

Not to mention the exorbitant costs.

"How did it happen?" Letitia asks eventually.

Natalie had already told her about the assault. What she was asking was *why*. But somewhere deep inside, she already knew the answer.

Natalie had stared at the road, her chest tightening the way it always did when she thought about Alex. Her big brother, who was always looking out for her. Who was so optimistic, so joyful. So full of life.

When kids at school had teased her, or tried to push her around, he would appear as if by magic, shoeing them away without fear or anger. He was quiet, but big for his age. Usually, though the boys taunted him, they weren't physical with Alex.

"He was riding his bike home from school one day. I had stayed home sick. So he was by himself. One of our neighbor's kids was waiting for him. He always shouted at us, called us *monkeys*, or *abbos*, and told us to go back to where we came from. Which just shows how stupid he was. But anyway. Sometimes, he threw rocks at us. He'd do it in front of his parents, and they'd just laugh, like it was a big joke. My parents never confronted them. Just said that it was only names. Little stones. No harm done. That some kids were just mean. To try to make friends with him. Like you can ever be friends with a person like that."

Silence had filled the car, with all the things that could be said in that space. How even twenty-odd years later, Letitia's experience wasn't so different. It wasn't quite so overt. But it was still there, nonetheless.

It wasn't until Natalie had stopped the car outside Letitia's sharehouse that she continued, still staring straight ahead. "This one day, Alex had stood up to Grant at school. Had made him look foolish about something. So Grant was waiting for him. He pushed him off his bike as Alex rode past. Then kicked him. In the face, the head, the body. He was a bloody mess by the time another neighbor saw what was happening and pulled Grant away. They were both only sixteen. Grant got a rap on the knuckles, basically. He said that Alex fell off the bike trying to run him over, that's why he beat him."

As if that would have ever happened.

"But Alex wasn't capable of even talking at the time, there was so much damage to his face and jaw." The bitterness and rage and hopelessness felt as intense to Natalie as she spoke the words as it had on the day it happened.

"No one came forward as a witness," she continued, still staring blankly in front of her. "The police were very lenient. Charged Grant as a minor. Called it a *schoolyard scuffle*. He didn't even serve time."

Letitia had reached out, gripped Natalie's hand.

They had sat like that quietly, for a while.

* * *

Today, Natalie ignores another booking request, her mind playing over Christmas, Letitia, Alex.

At the time it happened, her parents had tried to claim expenses through the state transport insurance scheme, but they had pushed back, armed with Grant's claim that Alex had been at fault. So all the medical and therapy expenses beyond Medicare fell to the family. Natalie had watched the bills come in. Her parents were well-off, and there was no question of Alex going without what he needed to function as best he could. But recovery was slow, and progress was slower.

And there was so much to learn about brain injury. For a while it seemed like he might be fine. When he finally went back to school, he picked up maths subjects like nothing had even happened. He chose physics for years eleven and twelve. He grasped complex problems and could work them out.

But then, as the years past, it became clear his social functioning was not developing. Behaviors and responses that you'd expect an adolescent to grow out of, remained. And despite how quickly he could learn new concepts, he just as quickly forgot them.

He was overwhelmed in loud environments.

His anger was fast and brutal, and functioned like an on-off switch.

His planning and problem-solving were very poor.

He started having seizures.

The appointments were endless. Upeksha left work to care for him. To learn the strategies. To help implement routines every day. To organize appropriate supports.

It was clear that Alex would not thrive without a lot of input.

Upeksha knuckled down and gave it her all.

Natalie is very, very grateful for that.

13

GRIFFIN DISAPPEARS OVERSEAS for five days in the New Year, and Natalie is at once bereft at his absence and confused about that.

She feels on edge, and puts it down to not having told him about the termination. As a new guy on the scene—she can't bring herself to even *think* the word *boyfriend* yet—she thinks what she decides to do with her body is none of his business. It doesn't even occur to her that her edginess is due to the fact that she has been upset, and shared it with no one.

That perhaps sharing her confusion and pain about the baby might bring her comfort of some sort.

Instead, she arranges to have lunch with her aunt, who happens to be in Sydney for the holidays.

Aunty She greets her joyfully. It's been at least a couple of years since they've seen each other in person, but once the main catch-up questions are dealt with (Natalie lying about work, of course), she launches straight into the reason she made contact, before she loses her resolve and plays by the rule that has been drummed into her since birth:

Don't ask.

Not that it's stated like that. Her parents are evasive, and respond in a way that ensures she feels uncomfortable, disrespectful, *bad* for asking.

Aunty She has only ever given her a warning look when she's edged too close to unspoken topics, and her love and respect for Aunty She have seen her retreat obediently at once. But today, she's spurred on by some kind of urgency. Perhaps it's losing the life inside of her; perhaps it's a need to create some order out of chaos. She can't articulate it to herself. All she knows is that it feels critical to her feeling better.

"Mum never talks to me about Sri Lanka. She evades every single question I ask. I just want to have some idea about where I come from," Natalie says. "Can you tell me about her life there?"

Shehara's wide smile fades somewhat. She gazes at Natalie, not speaking, her eyes taking on a faraway look, almost glazing over. Minutes pass.

Finally, Aunty She focuses back on Natalie. "She doesn't talk about it for a reason, Natty-Noo. She doesn't want you to have to live with that stuff."

"But it's like this whole part of my life is missing. I don't know anything about what made her who she is. I don't know why she's so blind to race. I know it must have been bad. But I just want to know where I came from. I want to understand our family more. Because I *do* live with it. She might refuse to talk about it, but I can feel it. I can practically *smell* it. It seeps out of her pores. Her whole life revolves around something she refuses to acknowledge, refuses to talk about."

Shehara shakes her head, her eyes filled with love and sadness. "I can't, Noo. She's my sister. But you're a smart girl. You can find out enough. You can get the picture."

"I've got the picture," Natalie says, frowning. "I want the details. I know it's awful. I know it will hurt. I just want to be able to feel closer to her. To know where she came from. To be able to connect with how she is. To understand why she's so...white."

"Why now?" Shehara asks, not blinking at the intended

insult, and Natalie knows she is not going to hear any details from her. Her face is warm and open, but what she's inviting is for Natalie to share what has brought her here, why she wants these answers now. In a way, it's too late, Natalie knows this. She's nearly forty. Her mother is not going to change now. She's not going to suddenly want to be closer. Closeness involves uncertainty. It involves dealing with somebody else's internal, emotional world. It involves messiness and risk and heartache and *loss*.

Upeksha is certainly not going to want to have anything to do with that.

Natalie knows this.

What she doesn't notice is that while she fights to extract this from her mother, she avoids it in every other relationship herself.

* * *

Despite her disappointment about that conversation, Natalie spends as much of the next week as she can with Aunty She.

She often wishes they'd lived nearby growing up, imagining big, warm family gatherings, laughter and stories. *Would her parents have embraced that, if it was just the way it was from the start?*

She finds it hard to believe they settled in different states and different cities, and doesn't really buy the explanation of job opportunities. In a new country, in a whole new culture, wouldn't you want to hang on to the few family members that you had?

Still, she doesn't pursue it. And though they don't talk about the past again, Aunty She is happy to talk about recent visits to Sri Lanka, what it is like there, the things she loves and doesn't love about it. In turn, she wants to be a part of Natalie's life, accompanying her to the gallery, drawing out of her deep responses to different styles and subjects. She's curious less about the art itself than what it means to her niece, and though she's there on a solo holiday ("Uncle Pu had no interest in coming!" she laments), she sees Natalie at least every second day. She even sits with her in the park one afternoon, handing her cheese on biscuits as she sketches, the silence long and comfortable between them, the warm sun on their skin.

By the time she leaves, Natalie feels nourished.

It's bittersweet, though, because it contrasts so starkly with how she usually feels after spending time with family. So as nourished as she feels, she is also left with a yearning greater than it was before.

14

THE MAN IS WATCHING.

Finally, it might be time.

It has never taken this long before.

He makes a mental note that Christmas is a bad time for sticking to routines. It's been hard to find the right day. But he hasn't rushed. Rushing is for losers. Rushing means mistakes.

But also: his work is worth the wait.

He watches the woman leave her apartment.

A tingle of excitement starts in his groin.

15

"What do you think about children?" Griffin asks suddenly.

Natalie jumps so much she sloshes her wine.

They're out at a fancy restaurant, enjoying nice wine, excellent views, and overpriced food. A waiter glides up to her with a fresh white napkin, surreptitious and silent.

"Why?" she says faintly, the fetus they co-created hanging there between them, weighing her down.

"Well, I guess I feel like there's not much time left for me. I mean, I know there is physically speaking. But in terms of when I think it would be good, I suppose. I don't want to be an old dad. And I'm guessing we're similar ages. So I wondered what you thought about it. If it was on the cards for you."

Natalie shakes her head, looking down. She stills inexplicably sad about the baby. That it is gone, yes—but even more so because of the abnormalities. It feels tender and heartbreaking and fragile and...needy. Like that little being needed her love.

"No. I've never wanted children. Not even when I was younger. It didn't seem like something I would excel at." Natalie looks back up, watching Griffin carefully.

"I don't think you have to excel. Isn't 'good enough' the modern catchphrase?"

"Well, I mightn't scrape in with those accolades, either." Natalie smiles ruefully and shrugs, resumes sipping her wine. "My parents were...different," she says, her face neutral. "They were very focused on what they wanted for us, rather than what we needed. I feel like something got lost in the process. I just don't feel very maternal or like I could cope with children. All their needs."

Griffin nods thoughtfully. "Okay," he says, shrugging, picking up his fork.

Natalie waits. For him to declare she's not the right woman for him, for him to criticize her lack of womanliness, for him to list all the reasons she ought to want children, the way that most people do when she drops that news on them. Even strangers try to tell her that she doesn't know her own mind, and that of course she wants them "deep down," or that she'll "regret it one day."

But Griffin moves on to another topic, as intense and interested in her thoughts on the next subject as ever.

Eventually, she can't help herself: "What about you? And children?"

He finishes chewing his mouthful slowly.

"I always thought I'd like to be a dad. It seems like what everyone does, you know? You have fun, you establish your career, you settle down and have a family. And if I was with someone who really wanted kids, I think I'd be into it. Excited, even. But it's not a deal-breaker for me, if that's what you're wondering." His eyes are very dark as he looks at her, and her heart starts thudding in her chest.

She gulps a mouthful of wine and hastily looks away.

* * *

Later, wandering the streets of Sydney CBD, Griffin continues to be a little too good to be true.

He tells her about his childhood: He had grown up in a small country town outside of Melbourne. The type of rough country town that sneered at difference and punished it liberally. The type of place that Natalie would have enjoyed growing up in even less than where she did.

There were no people of color at his low-achieving public high school, and in the seventies and eighties he was still taught a curriculum that either omitted anything about Aboriginal and Torres Strait Islander people, or if it did mention them, referred to them as hostile and violent, and the First Fleet as brave heroes taming a wild, unknown land. It was only through his own passion for travel that he became truly educated about other cultures, including his own.

It had been an embarrassing interaction with a passionate Irish backpacker that had set his education on the right path, her rage that he had no idea about Australia's colonization and treatment of Aboriginal people initially motivating only in as much as he wanted to sleep with her. But once he started reading he found he couldn't stop.

He spent his twenties travelling the world, working in bars, sleeping with backpackers. By the time he returned to Australia, he spoke four languages well enough to get by, had a business plan that made him very wealthy over the next decade, and was plagued by an unshakeable sense of despair.

The world he had seen was beautiful beyond compare, and cruel beyond any comprehension.

His parents had been rough around the edges, but possessed boundless love and kindness. Everyone was treated with respect in their family, from the garbage truck drivers to the fancily dressed ladies behind the glass in the bank, where they went every week to deposit a dollar or two into the kids' savings accounts on their way to the library.

Everyone was treated as valuable, but children in particular were treated with reverence.

So when Griffin saw starving children in Rwanda, or children fleeing violence in Syria, then held in offshore detention by Australian governments for years at a time, sewing their lips together in protest, his heart was bruised in a way he felt he would never recover from.

He probably wouldn't be able to articulate it well, he said, *but when he saw Ivy that day in the gallery, staring at Jack Charles, the expression on her face spoke directly to his heart.* There was something in her demeanor that left a lump in his throat. And while he'd never had a problem approaching women ever his whole life long, somehow he felt too emotional at that moment to speak to her.

Seeing her again the next day had indeed felt like a sign to him.

His words wash over Natalie, comforting and intimate. She starts to dare to think she could lean toward him.

That perhaps she might be able to trust him.

That being with him might be okay.

More than that: that closeness to someone might be worth it, even.

However, just as Natalie starts to feel this opening, this blossoming in her chest, her mother rings.

Fucking universe, she thinks.

She hesitates, then puts her phone away.

So she doesn't learn about the dead black girl found in the park near her parents' house for another whole day.

16

Natalie rolls over and curls into Griffin, still half asleep.

A delicious dinner, followed by hours of sex—the type of sex that you only have when you've just met someone and you wake each other up all night just to touch each other again. And again.

And on top of all that, cuddles against his delicious chest in the morning.

And yet, she still feels uneasy.

The perfection of him is hard to believe.

He sees me, she had thought to herself the previous night, astounded. Grateful.

But this morning, it all seems far too good to be true.

She doesn't understand that sometimes experiencing something different to what is familiar makes it feel wrong...even when it is what has been missing all along. As a child, she never learnt how to be vulnerable and rely on others. Somehow, she knew that it was critically important to her parents that she be "okay." That she not need too much or ask for too much or show too much vulnerability.

So Griffin looking at her and sharing himself with her and

trying to see who she is, is so unfamiliar that it feels catastrophically wrong.

In an intellectual way, Natalie understands parts of that. She'd read as much as she could about the conflict in Sri Lanka. She'd read up on intergenerational trauma and had made some sort of peace with how her parents had parented her. Given what they'd likely experienced.

In some ways, she knows that they did the best they could.

But their best wasn't good enough for her. She didn't get what she needed to thrive. And it was hard to pin down. You couldn't form a narrative around it that was linear and neat, where A led to B which resulted in C. Trauma was slippery like that. It wasn't a complete memory, stored with all the others. Terror and fear and silence in parents manifest themselves in children in complex and insidious ways. Ways that Natalie did not understand and could not articulate. They manifested in her body, emerged in her dreams, played out in her habits. Habits the unaware might consider quirks, something charming. But they were not quirks and they were not charming. To Natalie, they felt more like insanities.

So it was hard to tell herself a story that made sense. *My parents were traumatized and weren't emotionally available to me as a child, so I find it hard to trust in relationships,* is probably as far as she could take it, if pushed on the subject.

So now, lying beside Griffin, she feels the strong discomfort that comes with vulnerability—of opening yourself up to another human being. But she feels it in her body as something being wrong. She feels it as danger. So she lies there, overcome by the desire to flee, unable to link this instinct with the intellectual idea that it's simply unfamiliar to her to experience intimacy. To let her walls down, even a little. To not shut someone out.

However, she doesn't get a chance to flee, or to untangle these feelings and thus decide to stay. She's pulled out of this process by her phone ringing.

It's only quarter past seven in the morning.

Natalie frowns and reaches over to her bedside table.

Upeksha, again.

She declines the call, frowning. But a minute later when the phone rings again— her frown deepening in the interim—she hastily answers it.

Griffin, woken by the ringing and Natalie pulling out of his embrace, watches as her face falls.

"No, no," she whispers. "It can't be." But he can tell from her expression that it is.

"Let me call her. Let me google. I'll call you back."

Shakily, Natalie goes and gets her laptop, slipping back into bed, still naked. She looks stunned, and moves slowly.

"Ivy?" Griffin asks softly. He looks like he wants to help, but is not sure what is happening.

Natalie taps into the keyboard. She doesn't look up at him.

She pulls up a story on the ABC's website.

And there she is.

Letitia.

Smiling.

Stunning.

Reported dead.

17

THE PICTURE IS a couple years old. Natalie recognizes it from Letitia's bedroom. It's a picture of her at a university pub crawl, one night when she'd just made new friends in a new city. Letitia's smile is wide, her eyes laughing. Her hair is shorter, framing her face neatly. She looks young and carefree.

There is not a lot of information.

Twenty-three-year-old engineering student Evelyn Weber was last seen on Thursday, February 1st at around 8 a.m. She is believed to have been travelling to Linfield to visit friends. Police are not releasing any details of the case but are treating it as a homicide. Anyone with information is urged to call Crime Stoppers on...

Natalie feels numb.

She doesn't know why her friend would be visiting her parents.

She doesn't know why anyone would kill her, either. Escorting has its share of dangers, but she was making a social visit, not working, if her mother is correct about her destination.

Is it a coincidence that she had just told Letitia about Grant Boyd?

Is it a coincidence that Grant Boyd has just been released?

"It's her," Natalie says, her mother picking up on the first ring.

Her voice is lifeless. She feels sicker than she has ever felt in her life.

"I don't know," she says after a pause. "Maybe she just went by Letitia. Maybe she liked it better." Another pause. "I'm coming over."

Natalie ends the call and stares at Griffin blankly. She can't actually compute that this is happening. Walls are clanging shut all around her heart.

She doesn't feel like crying.

She feels like killing somebody.

18

RAVI AND UPEKSHA are staring at the television, side by side, their backs unnaturally straight.

Natalie gently takes the remote from her father's hand and mutes it. She sits opposite them, where she can't even see the screen.

Alex isn't there, and Natalie can't hear any evidence of him.

"Where's Alex?" she asks softly.

"Playing computer games in his room," Ravi tells her. "We gave him some extra time so we could watch and decide what to do."

"You haven't spoken to the police?" Natalie is surprised. She had thought, as good Australian citizens, that that would have been the first thing that they would do. Before even calling her, perhaps.

"We weren't sure..." Upeksha's voice trails off. "The different name..."

"When was she meant to come here?"

"Thursday for lunch. Such a lovely girl. She had sent us the most beautiful thank-you card for having her for Christmas. And emailed us a recipe she thought we would like. From her mother!

Such a thoughtful girl. We invited her to lunch and she accepted..."

Natalie is dumbfounded. Firstly that they were touched by receiving a Jamaican recipe—she supposed that was what it was —but mostly that Letitia hadn't mentioned the lunch date.

Was that strange, befriending her parents?

"You should call the police. Crime Stoppers. That number."

Ravi nods. He has already written it down, the pad and pen resting precariously on his knees, which are squeezed tightly together. He reaches for his phone and keys in the number.

Natalie and Upeksha stare at each other.

Still, Natalie can't cry.

She is too full of rage. Already, she's convinced herself that Grant Boyd is responsible.

She imagines Letitia walking up their neat, all-white street from the bus stop on the main road (she had resisted getting a car, content to utilize the public transport system, even to see clients in the suburbs).

She imagines her long black hair, her glossy, velvety skin.

Her white teeth and her big smile.

She imagines Grant Boyd, seeing her out the window. Or driving past her in his ute, perhaps.

She can't imagine what happens next. Her mind won't go there, can't.

She sits stiffly in her chair, her father's words faint in her ears.

"...on her way here for lunch...never turned up...thought she got caught up...young people these days...thought she got a better offer....we're just the parents of her friend..."

Though they're expecting it, the knock on the front door shortly afterwards startles all three of them.

Natalie jumps up before her parents have the chance. She opens the door to two men in plain clothes. They show her their badges, and she ushers them into the living room.

They ask lots of questions, directed at her parents.

Natalie keeps tuning them out, her thoughts jerking around erratically.

She can't bear the thought of Letitia being gone.

Her laughter, her down-to-earth attitude. Her understanding.

The way she lit up a room.

The way she just *got it.*

Natalie can't imagine she'll find someone like her ever again.

But more than her own sense of loss and grief and rage: she can't bear the thought of what Letitia endured before her death.

* * *

"How did you meet Evelyn?" It takes Natalie a moment to realize that the question is addressed to her.

"Through the student newspaper. She interviewed me," she lies.

She will have to tell them the truth. But right now, she doesn't want them to dismiss this as a sex job gone wrong.

"Did you know her as Letitia as well?"

"Yes."

"It's interesting..." one of the detectives tells her, cocking his head slightly. "You see, no one else has mentioned that. You three are the only ones."

Natalie frowns. She probably looks like she finds this information confusing, but she's frowning at them for chasing the wrong lead. She knows that once they learn how Letitia earnt all the money that is no doubt sitting in her bank account, they will quickly lose interest in the case.

A dead hooker is of little interest to anyone.

A dead *black* hooker? Well. She almost certainly "brought it on herself."

"Was she raped?" she asks, suddenly. She wants to change their line of thinking, but she also needs to know, in the horrible way that you know it will make it worse, but you kid yourself that the answer you're hoping for, however unlikely, holds the possibility of making it better.

She hears her mother suck in her breath sharply.

"That information hasn't been released yet," the detective says, looking at his notebook, glancing at his colleague.

"May I have a word?" Natalie asks, indicating the front door slightly.

She doesn't even know what she wants to say. But whatever it is, it's best said away from her parents.

One detective stays with her parents, the other walks into the front yard with her. Neighbors on both sides are watering their garden beds, as close as they can get to her parents' front door, curious about the well-dressed visitors. Natalie frowns at them, then indicates her car. The detective squeezes into the passenger seat, his long legs awkward in the small space.

She starts with Grant.

"Look, you probably know this. But a violent man has recently been released into number seven there." Natalie gestures to the house over the road. "He's been in and out of jail his whole life. And he violently assaulted my brother when he was sixteen, leaving him with a major brain injury. Alex still lives with my parents. He needs a lot of support."

The detective is not writing anything down.

"It was a racially motivated attack. He hated people of color living on his street. He taunted us for months before attacking my brother when he was by himself. It was very opportunistic."

Still the detective does not write anything down.

"I think you should look in to him first. He has the history. He has the motive."

"Miss Weber was sexually assaulted," he says, and Natalie jerks over the steering wheel, the pain hitting her in the stomach like the worst of her termination cramps. She expected this, but the confirmation of it is breathtaking. "I didn't want to distress your parents. And please keep that confidential at this stage. But it seems unlikely that a man who dislikes people of color would rape them, don't you think?"

Despite her anguish, Natalie feels a flash of rage again. The most basic education on the topic would teach an interested person that rape is about power, not desire. Surely a detective should know that?

"On the contrary," she says, her voice tight, thinking of the man who refused to pay, "rape is an excellent way to exert power over someone you despise. Just look at any war." She wants to add that perhaps the case should be given to someone with expertise in sexual assault as well as homicide; she can't believe someone so ignorant could be in charge here. But at the same time, she doesn't trust the police. She knows all too well the ways they entrap sex workers in South Australia, directing resources into sting operations against workers instead of targeting the dangerous clients who assault them. *As if sex work is ever going to go away.* And while she enjoys the luxury of decriminalization in Sydney, she doesn't want to exacerbate anything. She doesn't want this detective to feel he needs to assert his power about this case over *her*.

She stays silent and concentrates on breathing.

In, out. In, out.

"Evelyn was an engineering student," he continues, as though not hearing her. "She had just deferred her final year. Yet you said that you met her through the law newspaper. That she was interviewing you."

He lets the statement hang there. Natalie guesses that he knows that Letitia didn't transfer from law.

She weighs her options.

And dies a little inside.

19

ALONE IN IVY'S APARTMENT, Griffin takes a slow shower and wonders what to do next.

He had been planning on asking her about the different name on her mail this morning. But the turn of events had meant that question was left unanswered, still. And Ivy had shut down with walls so obvious and powerful she might as well have been thrown in a cell.

Of course, the violent death of a friend was awful. Horrifying. Vomit-inducing. But Ivy didn't express even a fraction of anything. She went very stiff, and very still, but she didn't cry. She didn't scream, she didn't collapse. She didn't want him to comfort her. She didn't do anything people usually do when confronted with something so hideously awful that life as you know it is forever altered in that instant.

In the shower, he leans into the heat and lets it pummel his face, run over his body. He keeps his eyes closed, memories like tiny chips of glass under his skin, scratching and pricking at him.

He remembers crying, and screaming, and collapsing.

He remembers life being altered forever in that instant.

He feels the pain like it is yesterday.

A thousand tiny needles stuck inside him, scratching him from the inside out, forever.

Subdued sometimes, but never, ever, ever destined to go away.

20

AS SHE HAS SUSPECTED he would, the detective closed his notebook with an air of finality when Natalie told him how she and Evelyn really met.

"You don't understand," she had insisted, her voice getting louder, it clear the detective was just humoring her. "She charges six-hundred dollars an hour. This isn't lowlife scum picking up a powerless woman off the streets and killing her for pleasure. She has good clients. She's fastidious about screening. She was just visiting my parents for lunch, for God's sake."

But he didn't seem interested in differentiating between the different types of sex work and the associated risks.

And Natalie was pretty sure he wasn't very interested in Grant Boyd.

This is where sex work stinks, Natalie thinks to herself. No matter how much she charges her clients, the general population curl their lips in distaste. There's no understanding, no belief that she and Letitia are just as nuanced a person as anyone else. Unless someone personally knows a sex worker and has their perceptions challenged, they assume all sex workers are less than human: drug-addled, desperate women who can't hold down any other work. Nymphomaniacs who could never keep a partner.

It was almost as though they thought that by choosing this profession, Evelyn was asking to die.

Natalie stays in her car, half defeated, half burning with white-hot, brewing rage.

21

THE MAN HIRES *a car at Melbourne Airport—a v8 ute, which suits his mood—and drives out to his family's old farm.*

His latest conquest has left him feeling unsettled.

Everything had gone to plan, of course. It always did.

But he feels uneasy nevertheless.

He doesn't know why he's taking this drive. If he tells himself anything, it relates to the solitude, the space to think amongst open fields. Driving has always soothed him.

He pulls up outside the farm two hours later.

The old gate at the start of the long drive has been replaced with stone walls with lions atop, and electric gates with sharp-looking tips on each black metal rail. The man supposes they are meant to look impressive, but they make him feel strangely wistful. He can't imagine why—his memories of living on the farm are hardly heartwarming.

Still.

He remembers racing to the bus stop on his bike, skidding to a stop at the gate, and hurling himself over it, his bike discarded where he stopped, despite the endless reprimands from his parents to put it out of sight and not block the drive.

He thinks he did that for a whole month before his father made sure that he never, ever did it again.

He sits at the gates, the engine idling. The plain trees lining the driveway are twice the size they were when he left. The house is blocked by high, neat hedges—another new addition from the new owners. His father moved into town several years ago.

The man has not visited his father in his new home.

If you asked him, he wouldn't have been able to explain why. He and his father were thick as thieves, he supposed you could say, after his mother left.

He stares at the gates, in his mind seeing her running through the orchard, laughing, the sunlight in her hair.

Her soft voice calling him over for freshly baked cupcakes.

The warmth of her smile, when his father wasn't around.

The man starts, a fleeting feeling confusing him, stabbing at him.

It's all okay, he tells himself, shaking his head as though to shake the discomfort away. The dead prostitute. It all went to plan. There's nothing to worry about.

It would not have occurred to him that that feeling might be what regret, or grief, or pain might feel like.

Regret and grief and pain were not part of his vocabulary.

He's tempted to go in, chat to the new owners, take a walk down the familiar dirt tracks. But he pushes that urge away too.

Nostalgia is also unfamiliar to him.

Instead, he turns the car around and heads back the way he came.

22

HER APARTMENT IS empty when Natalie returns home, and she's grateful for the solitude. She heads straight to her bedroom and sinks into her soft bed, pulling the second pillow in to her stomach to curl around.

The detective has promised to stay in touch, but she doesn't have high hopes for his investigation. He did, however—with the one flash of empathy he had shown the entire conversation—gently explain that Letitia's profession would probably be in the media soon enough. They wouldn't release the information at this stage, but at some point it might help them to have that angle when requesting information from the public.

"You might want to think about what you want to say to your parents about that," he'd said, and he had actually managed to look concerned.

Because, obviously, being a successful, self-employed sex worker was something to be ashamed of and to be kept hidden from one's loved ones at all costs, Natalie thinks bitterly to herself.

At the moment, though, that eventuality seems like the least painful thing to be pressing down on Natalie.

Her grief is quiet, and heavy, and colossal, and complex. It's not just that she loved Letitia. It was also that Letitia was a kind of home. She understood, experientially, how Natalie experienced the world. She understood her as an escort. She was one of only a handful of people in the world that Natalie felt effortlessly connected to. Who she could laugh about her parents with, and feel understood by. Her fierce protectiveness of them, alongside her abject despair at who they were and how they got there. The ways their experiences pressed into her, and changed her. Her resentment toward them and her connection to them, however dysfunctional. However damaged.

It's intermingled with a kind of hopelessness, because *do* black lives matter? Natalie feels this, rather than considers the question. She doesn't formulate sentences about it, but she feels it in every cell in her body. *Can a black woman just be plucked off the street with barely a ripple?* Because already, Natalie knows that there won't be marches thirty-thousand strong down Sydney's main streets. There won't be vigils attended by politicians and academics. There won't be cries of "things must change" echoing around the nation. Even before her work as an escort comes out, Natalie knows in her bones that for Letitia, this is true.

Curled up on her bed, her eyes dry, Natalie finds it almost humorous that she went to Aunty She about her parents. Like knowing about them would help her belong.

In Australia, suddenly and breathtakingly, she knows that no amount of closeness with her mother will help her to feel like she belongs.

23

---

*W*HEN THE MAN *returns to Sydney, his sense of unease hasn't lifted.*

He scans the news online, again, hoping to find something to settle him.

Following the story has never really appealed to him. He'd read things for a day or two, maybe a week at the most. But what happened, how people reacted, what the police thought—usually that stuff felt irrelevant to him. He felt invincible, untouchable. His plan was flawless, as far as he could tell. And he was still a free man, so it seemed that his assessment was spot on.

The police always looked for the disgruntled client. A job gone wrong. That was the beauty of his work. While they were looking at the movements of recent clients, the client they were on their way to and from, or looking for men who'd been sighted in the vicinity—the opportunistic stranger—he was long gone.

But he'd made a mistake this time.

Evelyn.

He didn't know Letitia's real name when he chose her. He always took care to meet his targets when they were working. It was easy enough to arrange. Book an appointment, with an old phone that didn't have his name attached to it. Be a model client. Nothing memorable. Polite, vanilla, respectful.

Wait a few weeks.

Wait, and watch.

It had worked every single time.

They didn't usually remember him, when he first approached them the second time.

He'd remind them—the day, the hotel, something they'd said. Something unique and well-planned, because he needed them to remember.

He needed them to feel safe.

So they'd remember. At least pretend to be happy to see him. Give him a friendly kiss on the cheek.

It didn't matter. He didn't need them to be genuinely happy. He didn't see them that first time to create a lasting impression.

That was what the second meeting was for.

But Letitia hadn't been going to see a client. She'd been going to visit friends. And even though there was still the "stranger danger" narrative to fall back on, it was much less robust than the whole prostitute-with-a-client-gone-bad narrative.

The police would be starting with strangers sighted in the area. Cars noticed. Usually, his method results in them being tied up with the "bad client" red herring for the first few days. They fail to focus on asking everyone to remember every car they'd seen in the vicinity.

And by the time they'd cleared the clients his victim was leaving or en route to...well. People's memories were pretty iffy two, three, four days later. Whatever people wanted to think about their own memory, the way they saw things was overlaid with all sorts of stuff. What they thought they saw becomes confused when faced with law enforcement, who really, really want them to remember.

His mind drifts back to the farm.

In a rare moment of clarity, he wishes his memory was so fickle.

His mum. His dad.

He wishes he *didn't remember everything.*
Some things are better to forget.

24

GRIFFIN SITS ON THE PLANE, staring blankly ahead while his fellow passengers disembark.

"Sir?" the hostess asks him, when those passengers have all long gone, and still he stares.

"Right. Yes," he answers, smiling wanly at her, rising from his seat.

He hasn't been able to reach Ivy since that day in her apartment, when the news of her friend's death catapulted her out the door.

It seems to have catapulted her right out of his life.

Phone calls and text messages have gone unanswered for nearly two weeks. He's thought about dropping in, but he guesses that she is grieving in her own way, and might not appreciate him impinging on her space. He sent flowers instead, just reiterating how sorry he was and that he was thinking of her.

To be honest, he doesn't know how he can be close to her in that space, post-death. He feels angry and confused himself. It feels too close to him, raises too many painful issues that he felt were long behind him, but are now sizzling and sparking too close to the surface.

Perhaps pain never really goes away, he thinks to himself, as he walks to a waiting taxi.

He thinks back to his conversation with Natalie, or Ivy, or whoever the hell she is, the night before the death. *Maybe she's just collecting Natalie's mail,* he thinks to himself. *Or maybe she's lying about something.*

He knows that's a possibility. Because God knows, he lied enough that night.

He's lied enough his whole life.

Not completely. Not entirely.

Not about everything.

He's found fiction works best when you thread a little truth through it.

25

"I DON'T HAVE money for you."

Natalie stops her advance into the apartment abruptly.

She just barely stops herself from shaking her head in disbelief.

Her first client back at work, and it's a Time Waster.

She had thought he looked a bit too young and broke for this as he opened the door, despite the fancy apartment.

Strangely, she doesn't feel too annoyed, or like he might be dangerous, a thought that plays on her mind a lot these days.

In the last couple of weeks, she has reached out to the sex-work community in a way that she never has before. Starting out, she had taught herself what worked and what didn't in this job. What she needed to do. How to stay safe. How to recognize STI's and dodgy clients. She barely spoke to any other escorts at all.

But after Letitia's death, she felt so alone and so lost and so angry, and had so few people to talk to, that she couldn't really think of anywhere else to turn. Eloise tried to help as best she could, of course. But for the first time, Natalie longed to connect with more people like her. Who understood what it felt like to not be taken seriously. Who understood being reviled and rejected for the work they did. Who *lived* it, just like her.

The community was open and welcoming, with various online groups, helpful advice, and all sorts of interesting commentary. Natalie suddenly wished she hadn't been so solitary when she started—a community like this could have saved her so much time and heartache.

Plus, she *liked* these people. They were smart and funny and strong. The more she chatted, the more she read, the more stories she heard, the more proud she felt to be counted among their numbers.

Nevertheless, she got straight to the point. *Her friend was dead. It did not seem to be a sex-work-motivated attack. She was out on a social visit. The police aren't taking it seriously. "Just a dead whore who picked the wrong client" kind of attitude.*

The response was overwhelming. Support, of course— kindness and rage and genuine understanding. But also practical tips—names and numbers of detectives who had been helpful for other escorts. Grief counsellors who were sex-worker friendly and knowledgeable. Useful suggestions and offers of help for general work administration to lighten her load while she was grieving.

But more than that, something else stood out.

Going through all the replies, the knowledge, the tips, something was niggling at Natalie that she couldn't put her finger on.

Something important.

And finally it hit her.

Wait, wait, WAIT, she types into one of the groups. *Are you telling me that between you, you know FOUR OTHER ESCORTS who have been murdered in the last two years with no convictions??*

Doesn't that seem odd to you???

She'd called one of the detectives suggested to her—Detective Casey—immediately. She hadn't expected her to answer, had her message all ready to leave on voicemail. When she answered, Natalie was momentarily taken aback.

"Hi, detective. My name is Natalie. An escort who was a friend of Minna Francis's gave me your number. You were investigating her murder a year or so ago."

"I see. Yes, I remember the case. How can I help you, Natalie?"

"I spoke to Detective Burns a month ago about the murder of another escort. Evelyn Weber. He wasn't very interested in the information I provided. It was suggested you might be more open to hearing from an escort."

The detective had only missed half a beat. "Of course. Do you have some information that you think might be helpful?"

"Yes," Natalie had said firmly, though she felt idiotic. She had suddenly realized how crazy her theory sounded. "My friend was not on a job. She was visiting my parents. We were...close. The detective thought she probably picked up a last-minute client, but I think that is extremely unlikely. Impossible, actually. I know her well. We screen carefully. We request at least twelve hours' notice." Natalie had stopped, the incorrect tenses hitting her hard. Hurting her. She had taken a deep breath. Continued in the past tense.

"Evelyn made good money. I'm sure she wouldn't have taken a last-minute booking, and I'm sure she wouldn't have just not shown up at my parents' without letting them know the change of plans. She was very polite, respectful. My parents are quite elderly. She would not have disrespected them like that. I don't believe that is what happened."

A pause.

"I see. And what do you believe happened?"

Natalie had swallowed and gripped the edge of her table.

"I connected with some other workers after her death. And I learnt that there have been similar deaths. Four other escorts, all on their way somewhere that they never arrived to. All murdered and their bodies found outdoors. No one has been arrested for any of the murders."

There was silence on the line. Natalie had hurried to fill it, before she could be dismissed.

"I think a killer is targeting escorts. And there's a guy...near my parents. He's been in and out of jail his whole life. He attacked my brother and left him with a brain injury. I just wanted to make sure he's being looked into. He was right there. Near Evelyn that day."

Afterwards, Natalie had slumped on her sofa. *What does it matter?* she had thought to herself. It might stop Grant killing other escorts, but it wouldn't bring Letitia back.

* * *

"Ah...Ivy?"

Natalie was miles away. She focuses again on the young man standing in front of her.

He can't be more than twenty-five. He has shaggy, dark hair and an irreverent grin. Under his tight, faded black tee shirt, she can see the definition of his abs.

Part of a tattoo curves out from the sleeve across a tanned, solid arm.

He looks confident and relaxed.

Natalie, normally so immune to the charms of men, finds her eyes wandering.

He's ridiculously good-looking.

She knows, from experience, that that means he's probably horribly entitled and a terrible lover. But her eyes roam over his arms, his stomach anyway.

"No cash, no loving; sorry, Aaron. Call me again when you're flush."

"No, wait. Please. I don't want sex."

Natalie rolls her eyes at the lifts, which she has turned back toward in order to disappear into. *Great,* she thinks. *Another one who wants to talk and thinks that's free.*

"Well, if you just want to chat, you can pay my social rate, it's a bit less. Would that work for you?" she says sweetly over her shoulder, her legs still facing definitively toward her exit. At least he had paid a deposit to cover some of the wasted time.

"I saw you. In Sydney. At the gallery."

Natalie turns slightly. She frowns, her spider sense kicking in, suddenly on high alert.

"I don't have 'sex worker, here's my website' printed on my forehead," she says carefully, backing away a couple of paces into the muted light of the landing. The extra distance is hardly more comforting, though; the apartment block is stunning, and deserted. She can't even *hear* evidence of anybody else.

Through a huge glass window at one end, she can see boats and surfers dotted across the bay.

"I have, ah...looked at advertising sites now and then," he says, looking at her under long, black lashes. He looks like an enthusiastic puppy, excited and unabashed.

"So you saw my picture and recognized me from the gallery... and decided to book me...for...?"

"A date."

"They involve cash."

He looks around, amused, suddenly aware of being in a public space.

"Please come in," he implores. "I mean I *have* money. Or rather, my brother does." He chuckles to himself, then sees Natalie's look of alarm. "He's not here, don't worry," he hurriedly assures her. "No gang bangs with my brother, I promise." He shudders to himself, his face contorting with some kind of comical horror. "Give me ten minutes. I'll transfer you the money for the hour if you want to leave after that. But I think you'll want to stay." He saunters back into the apartment, leaving the door open, unbelievably cocky even for an attractive twenty-something-year-old.

Despite herself, Natalie wants to follow. Her alarm has evaporated. Partly, she trusts her gut in relation to sex work, and she thinks she is safe with this...boy. Partly, she's curious to see just what someone so young and inexperienced thinks he has to offer. At least it will be amusing to share with her newfound whore-friends. *This twenty-year-old man-child tried to convince me to stay for free by showing me what he thought was an impressive cock!* she imagines chortling to them later that night.

If she's completely honest, part of her, too, wants to wander along behind his arse, admiring his shoulders, the way his jeans hang off his hips. He looks like he could be a cowboy, or a surfer, or maybe Brad Pitt in *Thelma and Louise*. And the stirrings of interest are a nice change from the despair of the last few weeks. The pain of it.

So she walks into the crisp, white space, the interior every bit as luxurious-looking as she expected from the fancy lobby and the prime location. A series of small, beautiful artworks are tastefully arranged along the hallway, understated and brilliant. Despite herself, she pauses in front of them, sucking in her breath.

"In here," her client calls from farther inside.

Turning toward the living area, with its pristine white couches and inviting shaggy, white rug, though, it's not the killer view that stops her dead.

26

ON THE DAY the man's mother left, it was the smallest act of self-protection that dictated who left, and who stayed.

If he ever thought about it, that might have seemed unfair. That he was only trying to protect himself, and he ended up the least protected of them all.

Catelyn.

Back then, the little light that flickered inside her—the flame burning brightly that had perhaps drawn his father to her in the first place—had not gone out completely.

When her husband was at work in the paddocks, she could relax and play with her children. She wanted them to know love. She wanted to see their faces bright with joy.

She always knew when her time was up: she could see the dust rising from the approaching tractor or ute, hear the growling engine coming closer. In the fifteen or so minutes between her becoming aware of her husband returning home for the night, the day's work done, she diminished in ways her children could see perhaps even more clearly than she could see herself.

And they retreated, torn between a desire to protect her and a desire to not see.

It was not that her husband was routinely violent. Just that she now knew that it would come again.

It always did.

The man shakes himself. He does not want to think about that day.

On that day, he was powerless.

He was powerless for the entire three years that he didn't see his mother.

But he hasn't been powerless for a single day since then.

27

THE PAINTING IS ALMOST LIFE-SIZE.

It dominates the room not merely through its color: the woman depicted is a physical presence. She's so vivid, so detailed that she almost steps off the canvas and into conversation with Natalie and Aaron.

Despite the angle, Jack Charles is easily recognizable. He appears exactly as he does in the award-winning portrait, except where the frame ought to be, he fades into dark swirls. He looks like a ghost, or an apparition, or a dream.

In the picture, Natalie recognizes everything she was feeling in that moment. She's wearing a simple blue dress. Her hair is in its natural state, unstyled and sticking up in random directions. One hand is lifted to Jack's face, though Natalie knows she did not do that in the gallery. But the gesture perfectly reflects her longing, her confusion. Her pain.

She looks ethereal. She looks, indeed, like she wants to morph into the apparition before her and float away.

But as those words come back to her, other things start to niggle and stab at her, too.

Dead sex workers.

Her short, short hair.

Natalie spins away from the lush white rug and vomits all over the wall behind her. For a second, she watches the evidence of her distress sliding down the wall and pooling on the floor.

Then her legs slip out from underneath her, and strong arms reach out to catch her and save her from crashing to the vomit-covered floor.

* * *

"Hey there."

The client's voice is soft, his fingers gently stroking her hair.

Her head is in his lap, and she is looking directly up at him.

Panic.

Natalie scrambles up and away from him, her eyes wide. But he only looks worried. "That wasn't quite the effect I was going for," he tells her, his eyes still dancing, despite their concern. "I thought you might swoon at how clever I was, and agree to a lunch date some time. Fainting, maybe. But vomiting? No. I didn't consider that as a possible response."

"Why did you paint that?" Natalie whispers, though she knows what he is going to say. It's written all over the damn canvas.

"You looked so haunting. So beautiful. So sad. I felt like two hundred years of race relations were captured in your face."

"I sat and stared at you for a while," he continues, watching Natalie with concern. "It was probably kind of creepy, actually. I was picturing how I'd paint you. I didn't even notice you'd left! I ran around the gallery like a lunatic. I even asked the girl at the front desk. But all I could think to say was 'the one who was staring at Jack Charles like she wanted to morph into him' to describe the person I was looking for." His eyes crinkle, laughing at himself. "Needless to say, she thought I was nuts. She just side-

eyed me with the 'I'm-dealing-with-a-crazy-here' look on her—
hey, hey, what's wrong?"

But Natalie is gone.

The front door clicks gently behind her, the soft-close feature
at odds with the forceful urgency of her exit.

Aaron stares after her without moving for a long, long time.

28

O*N THE DAY his mother left, a parcel had been delivered.*

Brian had drunk too much the night before. He wasn't a big drinker, and the violence wasn't tied to alcohol alone—but when he did drink, the aftermath lasted for days.

The parcel was a part his father had been waiting on for the tractor. A piston, perhaps, or maybe a carburetor?

The deliveryman had chatted for a minute, and Catelyn was brighter than usual, lest he smell the tension in the air, detect the unhappiness that rolled off them all in waves. In a way, she was trying to protect Brian. Or maybe she was trying to protect herself—was she more ashamed for herself, or for him? Did she not want the community to know that he was violent, or that she suffered it?

But Brian, hungover and blind to this, hissed only "Slut" as she walked back in from the front door, shoving her against the wall almost absentmindedly.

The thud seemed obscenely loud in the quiet kitchen. Catelyn slid down the wall to the floor.

Three small pairs of eyes fastened upon her from the breakfast table. Marilyn's filled with tears. Brody's dropped immediately back to his cereal, the struggle within him working on his face. The desire to go to her; the fear of the consequences. He'd tried to protect her in the past, and it had only made things worse.

Catelyn staggered to her feet. She needed the children to know she was okay, so they could stay seated, get ready for school.

So Brian wasn't provoked further by them trying to help her, which enraged him.

But Brody, sensitive and pained, seemed to have come to a decision. The eldest of the three, he felt that if it was anyone's job to protect his mother, it was his. Loathing and fear toward his father simmered underneath his tiny frame, showing through as defiance. He stood up slowly, the chair screeching on the worn lino floor.

Everything looked as though it was in slow motion.

Brody standing up.

Brian turning toward him. His features transforming into fury.

Catelyn tried to lunge forward, but as though she was in one of those dreams where your feet seem stuck in treacle, none of her limbs moved fast enough.

Brian's hand moved up and across his chest and in front of his face.

Brody took a step toward her.

Brian's hand came back down, so slowly in Catelyn's mind that for a second she thought that it would land softly, like a pat.

The crack as it connected with the back of Brody's head was shocking.

He dropped to the floor without a sound.

29

FOR THE REST of her Melbourne tour, Natalie is on autopilot.

Part of her is conscious of the things that need to be done—hair, makeup, clean lingerie, changing sheets, being delightful—but if anyone had asked her for a single standout detail of her bookings, she would have been lost.

Finally, ten-thousand dollars richer and ten-thousand times more worried than when she left, she boards a flight home.

Eloise picks her up from Sydney Airport, and they drive in silence to Eloise's flat, where Eloise regards Natalie carefully.

It's nearly nine o'clock. For the first time since she fled Aaron's apartment, and his painting of her, Natalie starts to let her guard down.

Nursing a Shiraz, she tries to calm her crazy heart. She doesn't know how it hasn't been lurching half out of her chest and scaring her clients for the entire tour.

Taking a deep breath, she tries to explain her jumbled thoughts to her friend.

"Griffin. He approached me on the street. Said he'd seen me staring at the Jack Charles portrait the night before. He said something virtually identical to what this client said to me in

Melbourne. He'd painted a picture of me looking at Jack's portrait. But they said the *exact same things*. About me looking like I wanted to morph into the picture. Like, that's a weird thing for one person to say, right? Two people?"

Eloise nods, placing a hand over Natalie's to still its worrying at the tablecloth.

"But the picture made me remember...Griffin met me all dressed up as Ivy. Whenever I see him I still wear one of my wigs, most of the time. But in the picture...I'm in casual clothes. With no wig. No makeup. I don't really know that he would have recognized me from the gallery...would he? It's bothering me. With all these dead escorts."

Natalie breaks off, putting her head in her hands.

"God. None of them were killed in a booking. The last client they saw and the one they were going to visit all had alibis, CCTV, something that cleared them. The police haven't put a lot of resources into any of them. They're considering them last-minute bookings gone wrong. But just say. Oh, God. Is it Griffin? He was with me when they found Letitia, but not at her actual time of death. Am I being insane?"

"No. *No.* You trust your gut. If something feels off, it probably is. But what about this other guy? What if he's the off one?"

Natalie shakes her head slowly.

"No. He took me to his brother's apartment. He really thought I would be excited about the painting. I panicked and ran, but I think...the painting was so detailed. He really did see me standing in front of Jack's portrait. He got the look on my face fucking *perfect*. It looked exactly how I felt. How I feel when I think of that portrait."

"Maybe they work together?"

"But why? Why disorient me like this? It must have taken him days, maybe weeks to paint my portrait? Why would you bother? And that's pretty crazy evidence of a connection to have in your studio. Unless he burns it..."

The two women are silent for a while, staring at each other.

"Just go to the police. Get them to check Griffin out. You don't have to tell him. But..." Eloise studies Natalie's face. "Don't see him for a while, okay?"

* * *

For the rest of that night, back in her apartment, Natalie gathers information from her new friends.

Five dead escorts.

Sephora.

Catey.

Minna.

Kiki.

Letitia.

She asks if anyone knew their real names. If they had boyfriends. Even new ones.

She doesn't discover much. Like her, most escorts keep their private lives private. Even with her newfound camaraderie, Natalie has no intention of telling these women her real name, or real details about her life. She doesn't know their stories. And in Natalie's experience, untrustworthy people are statistically likely to be everywhere. Even in Facebook groups purporting to help people.

At about midnight, her work phone pings, and she stiffens.

```
Melb Aaron: So I guess you didn't like
the painting.
```

Despite herself, Natalie's lips twitch.

If she was going with her gut, she would say that this young man was optimistic but harmless.

Then she frowns. *But what did my gut say about Griffin? Nothing much at all!*

She doesn't really think that Griffin is a serial killer. Anyone who brings soup and watches *Buffy* with you can't be a killer, can they?

But she can't shake the unsettling feeling that something doesn't quite add up.

She hesitates, then texts Aaron back.

```
Natalie: Sorry. Some weird stuff going
on. It was beautiful. Can I buy it
off you?
```

She hits send, then immediately regrets it. Does she really want a reminder of those feelings taking up a whole wall in her tiny flat?

Still, she has bigger things to think about, and she pushes her phone aside and looks at her meagre notes.

Then something else occurs to her.

In her head, she can hear her mother clicking her tongue in frustration, but she types another message into the group anyway:

Were Sephora, Catey, Minna, and Kiki WOC?

30

CATELYN DROPPED to the floor beside Brody. Blood was trickling down her face from split skin on her temple. A dark purple blotch was already blooming around it.

Blood had also splattered across her bright yellow dress from Brody's nose. He was conscious, but so terrified and shocked he might as well not have been. His father had never actually hit him before. Shouted, cursed, pushed a little, yes. But a full strength, adult blow? No.

Brian sneered down at his other two children. "Which one of you two little pussies is going to come and help me fix the tractor?"

He was already walking toward the door, the parcel under one arm, not waiting for a response. Andrew pushed his chair back so sharply it cluttered to the floor.

"He has school!" Catelyn protested weakly.

Brian did not even pause on his way out of the house. And Andrew scurried after him.

Catelyn helped Brody into the ute for the school run. Usually, the kids caught the bus, waiting at the end of the drive, Catelyn watching them anxiously out the kitchen window. They looked so little, so vulnerable.

Andrew was already pulling away from her. Where Marilyn and Brody flung themselves into her arms, confusion and terror in their eyes, Andrew hung back. In some ways, it made her worry less for him. If he was Brian's ally, he was less likely to be his target.

But Catelyn also knew how quickly that could turn.

And in the long run, aligning himself with Brian would only ever lead to ill.

31

Melb Aaron: How about an exchange? The painting for a date? ;)

THE TIME STAMP is 1:32 a.m.

Me: You're a night owl, I see. Did you by any chance notice how much older than you I am? You should take someone more energetic out for a drink. Someone who can reply to your messages at 1 a.m.

Natalie is used to men wanting to date her. Often, they are clients. She wonders what it is. Why do clients want to date an escort? She's heard stories of escorts dating clients who eventually make them give up escorting. Do they just want the goods for free? Or is it the perfect image that they get used to? The plucked, waxed, made-up, blow-waved flawlessness that she's selling?

But no one can keep that up full-time. Sooner or later, the ordinary woman is going to show through.

Sometimes, Natalie wonders if she's doing women a disservice—promoting the idea that women are like this. Perfectly presented, insatiable for sex, accommodating men's every whim. She likes to reassure herself that the good clients— the ones she goes the extra mile for, and is happy to see again and again—are smart enough to know that it's just a service. They know the boundaries and they don't press against them.

It's the stupid ones you have to worry about.

She dismisses Aaron for the time being, turning her attention to a more troubling text.

```
Griffin:  Morning, Ivy. I'm in Sydney a
day early. I'd love to see you. I know
this is a very difficult time for you. I
just want to see your face. We'll do
whatever you want to do. Please?
```

She hasn't actually seen or spoken to Griffin since Letitia died. She doesn't seriously think Griffin is capable of hurting her or murdering anyone, and waves a hand in front of her own face dismissively when she thinks of her agitation over the past few days.

How silly, she thinks.

Still, the complex thoughts and feelings about the pregnancy, the wondering if perhaps being in a relationship might be worth it after all, seem empty and pointless again. How is a man, let alone a *white* man, ever going to understand how she feels about this?

She feels desperately lonely. Letitia is the one who would have understood, and she can't talk to her. The devastation every time she remembers that is crushing all the motivation clean out of her. She can barely force herself to cook a meal, let alone converse with people. But while she recognizes her loneliness, she doesn't recognize that her retreat back into solitude doesn't solve her problem. That what she's protecting herself from is not pain, but vulnerability. And you have to get close to people for them to support you in the way that she longs to be supported.

She doesn't see herself as a herd animal, wired for connection.

She thinks she's strongest on her own.

Feeling like it's all pointless anyway, she goes to send Griffin a message telling him she doesn't want to see him anymore. *What's the point?* is all she can think. But just as she goes to click on the message icon and compose something short and to the point, she sees she has ten new notifications in Facebook. She opens that app instead.

People have commented on her question.

She'd forgotten all about it.

As she scans their answers, her heart starts to sink.

32

EVENTUALLY, Natalie phones Detective Casey.

She'd ummed and ahhed, pulled her phone out, put it away. Pulled it out again and read Griffin's message fifteen times.

But she can't think clearly, and she doesn't trust herself to make a sensible decision.

After greeting the detective and an awkward pause, she launches into her concerns.

"I met someone recently. I know it sounds crazy. But I just want you to check him out. I know it sounds paranoid. But—"

Detective Casey cuts Natalie off gently. "Tell me what happened."

Her heart is beating too fast in her chest, her underarms clammy. She had half expected to be brushed off. Being listened to is making her even more nervous.

"A new client made a booking with me a few days ago. He told me on arrival he didn't want sex, he wanted to date me, and he showed me a painting he'd done of me. He'd seen me staring at a portrait in the Sydney Gallery. The painting was excellent. He's very talented. But when he was telling me why he wanted to paint me, he used the exact phrase that the guy I've been seeing used to introduce himself. That he'd seen me staring at the portrait of Jack Charles, that I looked like I wanted to morph into the painting. And that just seemed so odd."

Natalie's voice is high, her words rushing together, but she wants to get it all out before she's cut off. Despite the detective's gentle tone, she expects her status as an escort to reduce her credibility. And this story to reduce it even further, no matter what her gut says.

"And I realized, looking at the painting, that Griffin—that's the guy I've just started seeing—had introduced himself when I was dressed for a work appointment. With a wig on. So, long hair. All done up. Makeup. The full works. And in the gallery, I had no wig. My hair is very short. I had no makeup on. Something just doesn't add up. I just thought they might all be connected. It seemed like a chance encounter but...I thought..."

Natalie's voice trails off. It sounds threadbare at best. But the detective doesn't dismiss her.

"Look, it's not a lot to go on, you're right. It doesn't really warrant looking into him. But it does sound odd. So let's just see if anything jumps out at me. Do you have his full name and date of birth?"

"Griffin Edwards. That's all I have. About my age, so about 1980."

"No middle name? Or month of birth? What about an address?"

"No. Sorry." Natalie suddenly feels stupid. Griffin is an unusual name, but still. It's not a lot to go on.

She can hear tapping at the other end of the line. Detective Casey doesn't speak for a minute.

"Hmmm, you're in luck," she says eventually. "Unusual name. I only have three in Australia. Let's have a look. No, that one's too young, 1999. I have one born in November 1975. That would make him...forty-two. An address in Brisbane. Does that fit?"

Natalie turns this over in her mind. "He said he owned a

house in Melbourne, but he travels a lot for work. Lives out of hotels a lot. Wait, his phone number, would that help?" Natalie taps through her phone, then reads it out.

"I have nothing with that number coming up. Look—I need to go. But leave it with me. I'll look at the files of the other homicides against that number. What were their names?"

Natalie gives the detective the details she has gathered on the other escorts. She hesitates, then ploughs ahead.

"There's one more thing. All the dead escorts." Her voice catches in her throat. She struggles for a second, feeling like she can't breathe. Finally, she manages to get it out: "None of them were white."

There's the briefest of pauses. Natalie isn't sure whether she imagined it or not. All Detective Casey says is, "I'll have a look. See if anything fits. In the meantime, if you're worried, don't see this guy for a while, or stay in public places, at least. Keep safe. And keep in touch."

33

DESPITE THIS ADVICE, Natalie calls Griffin.

I'd know if he was a nutter, she reassures herself. *I've met enough of them to be able to pick them in my sleep.*

Still, she tries to remember the details of their meeting. The Uber prang—you couldn't fake that, she's almost certain. Sydney is too busy. There's too great a chance of getting stuck in traffic, losing sight of her. And what Uber driver would agree to it?

Then again, was Griffin in an Uber? She had assumed so, but perhaps he had a friend driving. He seemed to have enough money. Maybe a minor prang and the associated costs were peanuts in his world.

But even considering these ideas makes Natalie feel like she is losing her mind.

It's been a stressful few months, she tells herself. *The pregnancy, the self-doubt. The abnormalities.*

Grant Boyd moving back to Linfield.

Letitia.

It doesn't seem unreasonable to think the strain of it all has gotten to her. Her work means that she's always on edge, to some degree. That's how you stay safe. Escorts can't afford to be complacent.

What's not to say that it all just hasn't unhinged some screw in my mind somewhere?

But "morphing" into a portrait is a peculiar, particular phrase.

She keeps coming back to the fact that she hasn't heard anyone else utter it in the last twenty-odd years. Probably not since studying some obscure text in high school. It seems too unlikely that two men—both enamored with her—would use it to describe her in the exact same scenario, no matter how readable the expression on her face.

Something is wrong, and she doesn't know what.

But doing something is certainly better than doing nothing.

She can't wait around to see what a busy detective comes up with.

Also: she trusts her gut. Whatever's wrong, she doesn't think Griffin might hurt her.

It's too preposterous.

He's too thoughtful.

And the only way she can assess the situation further is by contact. So against the detective's good advice, she calls him anyway.

* * *

"God, I've missed you," is all Griffin says when Natalie opens the door to him. He pushes her into the back of it as she closes it behind him, his hands coming round her waist, his lips finding hers.

He looks tanned, and fit, and hungry for her. All Natalie's plans to talk go immediately to hell.

Afterwards, panting amidst tangled sheets, her brain tries to catch up.

She had *such* good plans. To keep her distance. To ask some questions. A flirty question about his birthday, at least.

But just like that first time, his sex appeal turned everything upside down.

She just couldn't think around this man. He was too sexy, too commanding, too *normal* to want to resist him.

And now, looking over at him, his grin wide, his eyes warm, she just wants to snuggle into him and let him take control of all things, not just sex, for a while.

She feels incredibly, incredibly tired.

"What shall we do this afternoon?" he asks, reaching for her, running his fingers across her stomach, lust already lighting up his eyes again.

"The gallery?" Natalie asks. "A walk in the park?" All the thoughts of the past few days have left her too agitated to be still. She wants something to do, something to look at. Something to discuss.

IN THE END, they go to the gallery. But Natalie realizes it's a nice segue into talking, anyway.

"How did you recognize me, after the Uber prang?" she asks, glancing at Griffin. "I didn't have a wig on in the gallery, when you saw me looking at Jack Charles. I was all dressed up, with hair and makeup, when you saw me on the street."

Griffin looks surprised, and doesn't miss a beat. "You still look the same," he says, watching her curiously.

"So I needn't bother with the makeup, then?" she teases, not entirely satisfied. Her makeup is very...thorough.

"No, you needn't! Not for my sake. You don't need it," Griffin says, still watching her closely. He looks earnest. "You're stunning without a trace of the stuff. Although I do like a bit of hair to tug on." He grins, suddenly pulling her close and tugging on her hair to expose her neck, which he kisses lightly.

Natalie swoons immediately, opening her neck up to him further.

God, this is ridiculous, she thinks. *It's only been an hour, and I already want him again.*

But she doesn't have time to think further, because he's edging her toward the toilets.

"We can't!" she squeaks, mortified. "People will see!"

"You should be more worried about them hearing, with the things I want to do to you," he growls in her ear, his voice so sexy, his desire for her so arousing that she actually can't help herself —she lets him direct her without resistance. He glances quickly each way outside the disabled toilet to check that no one is watching, then pushes her inside.

34

CATELYN WASN'T ALLOWED to drive the ute. Brian considered it a farm car, and insisted he might need it at any moment. On that day, though, she had eased into the shed, her shoulders hunched, her head lowered deferentially.

Instinctively, she knew that looking small and weak was safer for her.

"I need to take Brody to the doctor before school," she'd said quietly, eyes downcast.

"You hear that?" Brian had said to the boy, nudging him, all buddy-buddy. "That's the sound of whining that you'll have to get used to if you ever want to get yourself a wife."

The boy had nodded, latching on to the bond that Brian was offering him, believing, of course, at eight years old, that if he was on his father's team, he'd be protected.

"I'm taking the ute. I'll be back within an hour."

Brian had only grunted in response.

"Darling?" She had addressed the boy, pleading with her eyes. "You've missed a lot of school recently. Will you come?"

He had shaken his head at her. He thinks he remembers that day more clearly than any other day in his life.

"I'm helping Dad," he'd said. "He needs me." He remembers not looking at her. He still doesn't understand that it was easier to not care about her that way.

He doesn't know how Catelyn felt that day, because he never asked her.

He didn't know that his brother was waiting in the ute, holding a handkerchief to his broken nose. Though taking the ute was an unusual enough request that he must have understood that he was hurt.

Probably, though, he was focused on winning his father's favor not on the well-being of the brother stupid enough to provoke him.

He doesn't remember that she tried again, though. Softly. Pleadingly. Willing him to understand.

"He shouldn't miss too much school?" she asked, turning back to Brian. Trying. Wanting to take him with her so badly.

The boy had never noticed that she always made her statements questions when his father was in a violent mood; that she had found questions less likely to provoke him.

"You heard him, he's helping me!" his father had shouted, nevertheless. "Pay attention to what he wants, woman!" He'd thrown a bolt at her, not hard, but enough to make her flinch. "Silly bitch," he'd muttered, to no one in particular.

He does remember that she didn't take anything with her, anything that would have alerted them to the fact that she was going farther than the doctor.

He doesn't know that her plan—one she'd thought about and dreamed of a million times before—always featured three children with her. Never two.

He doesn't know how she hesitated with the key in the ignition, the battle that raged within her.

Is it okay to leave one child behind, to save the other two?

He doesn't know that she cried all the way to Sydney, the ute left outside the doctor's clinic, where they don't stop. She doesn't have much time, and there'll be doctors at the other end.

He doesn't know that he is in her thoughts, every day, for the next three years.

He doesn't know that she is consumed with plans of how to go back for him, or send for him, or send someone to just take him.

He doesn't know how terrified she is every night, images scrolling behind her eyes, of all the worst things she imagines happening to him. How she tortures herself, every single day they are apart.

All the man remembers is that she left him.

She took the others, and left him behind.

35

BACK IN HER APARTMENT, Natalie feels uneasy. The intensity of the toilet sex is making her squirm, and she can't quite figure out why.

At the same time, she feels horny as all fuck.

Griffin has insisted on coming home with her, saying, "You haven't replied to me in a month. Now that I've got you, I'm keeping you nearby for as long as possible."

They'd had dinner out, and sex again as soon as they were inside the door. Panting, frantic, fast sex. None of the slow, commanding, alpha sex Griffin had favored the first few times.

Again, panting in tangled sheets, Natalie tries talking.

"That was really hot in the toilets today," she starts, and he opens his eyes and rolls toward her.

"You have no idea how many times I've jerked off to images of taking you against a door like that over the last month," Griffin replies, smiling lazily. "There's something so hot about being somewhere illicit." He pauses for a bit, then adds: "There's something so hot about you. I've been pining for you. You have no idea. In fact," he reaches over and grabs her hips, pulling her flush against him, "I'm going to fuck you again in about ten minutes. I hope you weren't planning on leaving this bed any time in the next 24 hours."

Natalie laughs, despite herself.

"So is it just sex you want? Because we don't know anything about each other. But the sex is working for me, as it happens. I just felt pretty terrible after Letitia died." Even as she says the words, she can feel something inside her shutting down. Her face closes off, the sensation of feeling present and connected in the moment with Griffin, suddenly obsolete.

"Let's get to know each other, then," Griffin says, solemn. "What do you want to know?"

"Tell me about your family." Natalie snuggles into his chest, mainly so she doesn't have to look into his eyes. She feels guilty for trying to do some detective work, and tells herself it's just to help clear him so things can go back to normal. Whatever normal is for her.

She feels Griffin stiffen ever so slightly against her, but she just snuggles deeper into him. Though whether she's trying to reassure him or herself is unclear even to her.

"What do you want to know?" he asks lightly, his tone betrayed by the subtle shift in his body.

"About your parents. Where are they now? Do you still see them? Do you like them? I don't even know your birthday! Do you celebrate it with them?"

Griffin runs a finger lightly up and down the curve of her waist. His touch is gentle, reassuring.

"They're both dead," he says softly.

Natalie pulls away, leans up on one elbow so she can look at him, despite her guilt. "I'm sorry," she says. "You sound sad. You miss them."

"I miss my mum," he agrees, a troubled look in his eyes. Then they lock onto hers. "What about you? Tell me about your parents."

"Oh, God." Natalie collapses back against Griffin, despite herself. "I don't even know where to start. They're impossible."

"Yeah? How so?"

Natalie rolls over onto her back, her arm lying alongside Griffin's, lightly touching. She stares at the ceiling, wondering how on earth she can explain them.

"They fled civil war in Sri Lanka. They suffered there. Horrible things, that no one should ever have to suffer, I think. They're still suffering, but they pretend they're not. They've never spoken about it—to me, or a therapist, or anything. As far as I know. They just want to fit in to Australia. I call them coconuts. They've assimilated everything they can except their skin. They really believe that they are white. They raised me and my brother to believe that we were white, too."

Natalie pauses, remembering.

"I have this memory of complaining to my mother about being bullied at school. When she asked what happened, I told her, 'Nothing happened. It's just because I'm brown.' And she said, 'No. You're not.' And wouldn't hear another word about it. I'm still not sure if she was denying that I was brown, or denying that I was being bullied because of it."

Natalie is silent for a while, thinking how impossible it is to capture the essence of families to those outside them. Her family might be particularly troubled, but does anyone escape this? Can a nice white man from a loving family understand hers, even without the layer of race muddying the waters?

So to speak.

She cackles to herself involuntarily, and Griffin raises an eyebrow.

"Tell me," he says, but Natalie just shakes her head.

"It makes it very hard to develop a bond with someone, and trust them, when they refuse to see who you truly are," is all she says.

It feels easy to talk like this to Griffin. He is attentive and interested. But she wants to hear his stories, not share hers.

"Tell me about your mum. What do you miss? When did she pass?"

Griffin pulls her back in tighter, dropping a kiss on her shoulder.

"She was maybe the opposite," he says softly. "She made me feel like she could see me inside out, and loved me always anyway." He's quiet for a moment, then adds, "She was always baking. She was sunlight. Her smile lit up the entire world."

36

DESPITE HIS PROCLAMATIONS, Griffin doesn't even stay the night, claiming he had work to catch up on and that he'd call her later.

Natalie is grateful for the thinking space. And even further grateful when Detective Casey calls.

"Look, from our end, a Griffin Edwards of around that age and description doesn't exist. The guy in Brisbane is six foot six, not your guy. And the third one is visibly of ethnic descent, which doesn't match your description. Now, there might be a perfectly reasonable explanation about his nonexistence. Maybe he goes by his middle name, or maybe he has to be careful with his business and goes by a pseudonym socially, but hasn't legally changed his name.

"*But*—the phone number you gave us is a burner SIM, which isn't a good sign. People usually get those when they don't want to be found. It was purchased at a 7-Eleven in Melbourne CBD years ago. They've been phased out; you can't buy them without ID these days. What we can do is run it through our system to see if it was in the vicinity of the murder scenes. In the meantime, I would suggest exercising caution. If you must see him, do so in public places. Maybe—"

"He's had plenty of opportunities to kill me if he wanted to," Natalie interjects. "The killer seems to target the women when they're on their way to meet someone else. I guess it keeps him out of the picture. Maybe he..." Her voice trails off again. She can't picture Griffin intercepting someone with ill-intent. Not Letitia, not her.

She shakes herself. She needs to think about an unknown man intercepting Letitia. Did she catch the bus that day? Her Opal Card account didn't show her as catching public transport that day, according to the police. And Letitia was not the sort of person to fare evade. But then, Natalie knows that she herself has forgotten to tap on, on occasion. She catches public transport so rarely. But Letitia catches it all the time. It should be habit for her, routine.

"We don't know if Letitia caught the bus," Natalie tells the detective, and explains her thoughts about it. "She might have been intercepted between the bus and my parents' house. Or she might have gotten a lift with someone she trusted, who knew where she was going. No one has come forward, which could mean that person is the...." Natalie chokes on the word *killer*. She coughs. Continues. "Which means they planned it. Or maybe it was opportunistic. So if Griffin is...the guy..." If she can't bring herself to say *killer* in a general sense, there is absolutely no chance she can say it alongside Griffin's name. This whole conversation, as far as being related to Griffin, feels completely ridiculous. She wishes she had never mentioned the weird coincidence about the "morphing" sentence to Casey.

"So the killer was likely someone known to the victim. Maybe he was driving her to your parents' place, or intercepted her on the way. So if Griffin does pose a danger to you"—Natalie catches and is grateful for the less brutal turn of phrase, but it is still jarring—"he'll likely be taking you somewhere or intercepting you on your way somewhere else."

Casey considers this for a minute.

"So if that's the case, the police prioritize talking to the wrong people. Who the victim was visiting. Neighbors who might have seen a car or a stranger or a struggle. Descriptions of who was seen in the area at the time."

Natalie feels something like relief, but not quite. She can't put her finger on it. It's not just that she's being taken seriously. Some converging of that, appreciation for Casey's quick mind, and something else. The possibility of justice for Letitia not seeming completely impossible, perhaps.

"So if you must see Griffin, take some precautions. Going out anywhere, make sure he has no way of knowing your plans. If you see him in an unexpected location, don't get in the car with him."

Natalie starts shivering, despite the warmth in her apartment.

The wave of relief she had just experienced evaporates. Hearing it laid out like this, it all sounds very real.

Very plausible.

Utterly terrifying.

Someone is carefully planning and then killing escorts of color.

Should she just break it off with Griffin? Just to be sure? That seems like the sensible thing to do. But then, if it is him, he could still intercept her somewhere.

Or move on to someone else.

Some other brown escort.

Her skin prickles again. This time with a familiar rage.

* * *

Eloise comes over after work, which means it is late.

After Natalie has finished updating her on Detective Casey's information, Eloise berates her for meeting Griffin. Dismissing Natalie's proclamations of his innocence, she continues musing about him as though he is definitely the killer, and asks the question that even the detective had managed to avoid.

"But *why*? What is his motive? It's not like he's been rejected. Or maybe he went on a few dates with these women, and they broke it off with him, and then he killed them. But you think he's insightful and nice. Rich. Good lover. And he was seeing you long before Letitia died. I just can't get my head around why he would."

Natalie blinks. She doesn't say anything. She doesn't have the energy. She can't explain this to her friend.

To her credit, it wouldn't occur to Eloise that skin color might be enough of a motive. While some well-meaning people might claim they don't see race, Natalie knows that *not seeing race* is part of the problem, however much skin color does not factor into Eloise's judgements. Because while Eloise would never treat anyone differently based on their sexual orientation, cultural heritage, or even gender, probably—that also means that she doesn't really see the small ways that other people do. She doesn't feel the relentlessness of being seen as brown first. Seen as less.

She'd probably even feel like she understands. She's banging hot, especially in her office wear—a smart suit and killer heels. She'd have had different, equally unpleasant things yelled at her out of car windows.

"Nat?"

Natalie brings her focus back to Eloise. She thinks about all the men who hate women.

All the people who hate those with a different skin color to them.

She doesn't think Griffin hates either. She's almost one hundred percent certain that he does not.

But someone else?

Skin color and selling sex? Killer combo.

37

DESPITE ALL THIS, by the time she's slept with him several more times and he's flown off to China for a week, Natalie is hopelessly in love.

Her body is, at any rate.

She convinces herself that an unhinged serial killer would not invest this much time in a potential target. Months of kindness and good humor. It's almost laughable. She can't imagine what she was thinking. A word is, after all, just a word. *Sticks and stones...*

So when the detective calls her with worrying news—that the burner phone was in the vicinity of where one of the victims was found, in the time around her death—she is inclined to shrug it off as another coincidence.

"Look, I was wrong," she tells the detective. "I've been seeing Griffin for months. A nutter could simply not keep up a façade so believable for this long. I'd see glimpses of it at *some* time, I'm sure. It was just a silly coincidence that seemed important in my anxious state. I really think there's nothing to look into here," she continues. "In fact, can I withdraw my request and we just leave it alone, now?"

Though she thinks something doesn't quite add up, it's not *this*.

On top of that, the phone hasn't been linked to Letitia's whereabouts around her death. It was being used in Sydney, but nowhere near Linfield.

"It would have to match all five if we're looking at a serial killer, anyway, right?" she adds.

"That's the obvious thing to think. If this is the work of the same person, and they've managed to not get caught five times, then they're probably a little smarter than that," the detective responds. "I can't really do any more on what we've got. Call me if anything else comes up."

Privately, Detective Casey doesn't buy into Natalie's certainty that the whole idea was silly. People can hide all sorts of things for decades, with no one close to them suspecting a thing. If these deaths are linked—and it seems likely, with the murder method being the same in all five, on top of the target victims all being escorts of color—then the killer has worked hard to not leave any obvious tracks. Grooming a victim to set up the perfect crime is not a stretch at all to that end.

Still, there really isn't anything concrete to go on. Detective Casey thinks she will dig a little further, and keep in touch with Natalie. But there's no point alarming her further at this stage. And, if she's honest, no point in scaring a potential killer into hiding.

Natalie hangs up the phone, though, oblivious to all of this.

She doesn't feel worried.

She leaves it with the detective, and heads off to family lunch.

It's only in the car as she turns into her parents' street that she remembers Grant, and wonders if Detective Casey has followed up on that lead at all.

She feels a stab of anger at herself—for confusing the investigation with her paranoia. Looking into Griffin because he used a strange word seems ludicrous compared to Grant's form. She makes a mental note to call Casey back later.

Then she braces herself for lunch.

* * *

Family lunches have been quiet affairs since Letitia's death.

Natalie obediently eats everything Upeksha piles in front of her. Though she has no appetite, and feels sick with nerves most of the time, in her state of vulnerability she reverts to a childlike self, dutiful and subdued.

The gap between her thoughts and feelings, and her mother's understanding of her, feels wider than it ever has.

After lunch, she lies on Alex's bed, watching him through half-closed eyes.

She can hear her mother hovering at the bottom of the stairs, distressed that Natalie is in his bedroom again, but averse to calling her out of there even on a pretence, and upsetting Alex.

"Does it ever bother you?" Natalie asks, against her better judgement. She hasn't had a serious conversation with Alex since the brain injury. Like everyone else, she's tiptoed around him, not wanting to upset him. Not really fully understanding how his brain worked anymore.

Suddenly, she regrets treating him like a child for all these years. He was still in there, somewhere, her calm and steady brother. For a while, she'd tried to talk to him as she normally would, but it only ever confused or angered him. She gave up easily, she thinks now. She didn't work at it, like Upeksha did with all the other strategies she applied, day in, day out.

"They never stood up for you. They never so much as said a bad word about Grant. They never batted an eyelid about the whole fucking thing." The bitterness in her voice startles her. She knows she feels that way; she is surprised by her lack of control around her brother. If she wants to try harder to reach her brother, this is probably not the topic to start with. But she can't stop the anger seeping out. It's like honey leaking out of a gash in the honey bottle. Slow and unstoppable.

Alex looks up from the figurine he is playing idly with at his desk. His face is thoughtful, but he doesn't respond. And Natalie can't help herself; she just wants to talk. Talk to someone like her, who might get it. Sans Letitia, Alex's silence is like an invitation, a warm cup of milk before bed. Her words keep oozing out of her, hot and thick and sticky.

"They never wanted us to be brown. They try and try and try to be white, and they weren't there for us when anything happened that acknowledged our heritage. I felt invisible, not cared for by them. I know they loved us. I know they did their best. But it just wasn't fucking good enough. All these years later, I can't let anyone in. I don't trust that anyone will see me for myself and still care about me, and yes I do fucking well blame them. Kids need to feel that their true selves are seen and loved, bloody childhood development 101, how did they miss that memo? Why did they even have us if they hated brown people so much?"

Alex is gazing at her steadily now. It's Natalie who drops her eyes, not because she sees any judgement there, but because she wants to talk into a vacuum. She doesn't want anything reflected back.

"I never have relationships. I never trust that anyone will stick around. And our parents didn't even leave us! They just didn't make me feel like I was worthy, just as I was. Which was brown. They still don't want to know me! You know, I once asked them...I told them that there was more to me than what I shared at these goddamn family lunches. That I wanted to be closer to them. That I could share more of my life with them. I wanted to try to bridge that gap. See if, after all these years, they might see me and love me and we might have a fucking normal parent-daughter relationship. And do you know what they said?

They went off, and conferred, and came back and said, 'No thanks. We like things how they are.' Can you believe that? They want to just have these polite conversations about superficial things and they don't *care* who I am underneath that. And it's horrible and hurtful and painful and I keep coming back every two weeks, *why?* Even I don't know why. Why do I still come here?"

At that, Natalie flicks her eyes back to Alex's. She's not upset. Getting emotional is not something that occurs for Natalie. She's almost clinical, like someone studying this bizarreness from a place of detachment and curiosity. *Look at this interesting phenomenon! Let's have a little look at that! Poke it with a stick, maybe!*

Alex is quiet and still, a rare state for him. His silence is like a warm embrace. Natalie falls into it with more words.

"I've been seeing this guy. Griffin. He's lovely and thoughtful and kind and handsome. But I've been worrying that he's a serial killer. Because of a sentence he said. And I want to kill Grant. I want to kill him for what he did to you, for his casual, evil stupidity that cost you so much. I *want* him to be a serial killer, Letitia's killer, so I can fucking kill him. I want someone else to feel persecuted and out of place. Picked on. *Ruined.* I think I'm going insane. Sometimes, I want to kill our parents, too."

Until she says it, Natalie didn't even know that this was true, but in that moment she knows that it is the case. Not because she hates them, but because she can't reach them. They're her people, and they should "get it," but they don't. And the pain the separation causes feels as huge as murder.

For the second time since Letitia's death, she catches a glimpse of just how alone she feels.

"He's just the face of it," Alex says quietly, and Natalie stops, her mouth half open, another fierce spiel halted in her throat. She stares at Alex in surprise.

"It won't help," he goes on, his eyes steady on hers. "He's just one person. You won't feel better. The world won't be a better place."

Natalie swallows her surprise, leaps at the chance this conversation seems to offer her: normalcy, with Alex.

"I will feel better," she says, stubbornly. "The world will be a *slightly* better place."

"It won't help you," Alex says, shaking his head slightly, his gaze intense. "You didn't get the love you needed from our parents. You can keep that cycle going. Of fear, of scarcity. Being so afraid of love that you strangle it whenever it comes near you. Or you can open yourself up to love. That's the antidote."

And for the first time in as long as she could remember, Natalie starts to cry.

THE MAN IS ready for the next one.

Usually, he leaves it for months between conquests.

But his appetite is growing.

And he's decided on the perfect number six.

So perfect.

He messed up with Letitia.

He won't mess up with Ivy.

He can't afford to make another mistake.

She's snobby, this one, *he thinks.* Charges eight-hundred dollars an hour! Fucking grandiose whore. Who does she think she is?

Well, he'll teach her who she really is.

He'll teach her the lesson that all these whores need to learn.

39

"I NEED TO ASK YOU SOMETHING."

Natalie is lying in bed with Griffin, where they seem to be spending most of their time.

After a week away, he's basically hijacked her weekend again and kept her as naked as the temperature allows. He's managed to even make naked cooking seem sexy.

"This is uncomfortable. But when Letitia died, the police asked about you. We'd only seen each other a couple of times, so I didn't think it was relevant. But I gave them your name and number. And they called me later to say that you don't exist in Australia. And the number is a burner phone. They weren't concerned. You weren't a person of interest. But I'd like to know about your name."

"That's why you asked about my birthday back then."

He doesn't look cold, but he doesn't look warm, either.

She can see his brain ticking over. Thinking about what to say, maybe?

Finally, he looks her in the eye and grimaces. "I haven't been entirely honest with you," he says, and Natalie's heart jumps. The explanation. God, she hopes it is normal and valid and not completely insane.

"My family wasn't quite the way I described it." He pauses again, and Natalie waits, her body stiff, her heart in her mouth.

"My father was violent. My mother left with my sister and me when I was still in primary school. We changed our names. Well, our last name at least. To something nice and common. Edwards. The stuff about my mother was true. She was kind to everyone. We had nothing after we left, and she made us feel like we had the world. She taught me to look for the good in people, that everyone has something. And if you look first for the good things, you'll be closer to people. Happier, too."

Griffin looks wistful, his eyes faraway, torn between the loving memories and the loss of her.

"You really loved her."

"Yes." Griffin looks back at Natalie, and is silent for a while. Then he continues: "When she died, I was only just out of high school. We had nothing. I worked after school, and my sister had started doing some babysitting as well, but she was only fourteen. It wasn't going to work."

Griffin pauses again, clears his throat. He glances at Natalie sideways, his expression slightly odd. Natalie is certain he's not being honest with her, or at least is holding something back.

"Mum had had a hard life. Everything she did, she did for us. To give us a better chance than she had. The stupid thing was, after she died, I found her sister. She wasn't well-off, by any means, but she would have helped. I don't know why Mum never asked her. Maybe she was too proud, maybe she was too ashamed. But she never made contact with her. I sent my sister to live with her to finish high school, and packed a bag and used the last of our money to buy a passport and a plane ticket. I didn't come back to Australia for nearly ten years."

Minutes tick by. Griffin looks lost in memories. He looks haunted, and troubled, and full of pain.

"I go by Griffin, but it's not my birth name. I was named after my father. Not the same name, but similar. And I didn't want any part of anything to do with him."

"I'm sorry," Natalie says softly. She feels full of tenderness, alongside a nagging guilt that she ever thought to mention his name to Detective Casey. *This* explains her uneasiness. Griffin *was* hiding something, but because it was painful and personal, not because he was a bad person in any way. A childhood like that certainly makes it understandable to smooth over a few rough edges. So maybe he put a little too much thought into the happy family narrative he told her; maybe the lies did come easily to him...*but he's probably repeated that story several hundred times,* she tells herself.

She reaches for his hand, her heart bursting. But he pulls it away.

"I need to tell you something too," Natalie says after a while, breathing deeply and slowly, trying to calm her pounding heart.

Griffin rolls back toward her, raising an eyebrow in a question, but the gesture is mechanical. He looks tired and defeated. Natalie wonders if now is the right time, but she goes ahead anyway.

"I should have told you earlier. I didn't really expect us to get to this point..." Her voice trails off as she tries to pin down what this point actually is. A relationship? That's in with a chance?

"That first time we met...I fell pregnant. I've never wanted children. Like I said, my family...I just don't think I'd do a good enough job."

Natalie rolls onto her back to stare at the ceiling. She just can't look Griffin in the face right now.

"I was planning on having a termination. And at the last minute I had second thoughts. I asked to see the fetus. I heard its heartbeat."

To her surprise, a tear trickles out of the corner of one eye, and she brushes it away impatiently.

"There was something wrong though. The doctor told me it wasn't a viable fetus. That it would die anyway. And I was devastated. I still don't really know why."

Now fat, silent tears are rolling down Natalie's cheeks. She still doesn't look at Griffin, who gently reaches out for her this time. But she holds a hand up.

She wants to tell him the rest. The escorting. The loneliness. She feels so close to him in this moment. She believes he can hear it; that he will be compassionate, not judgmental. That he will hold space for her, rather than edge away from all her mess.

In a way, though, she's just desperate to know. To find out, for once and for all, whether this relationship has legs. Failing to acknowledge that sharing something so vulnerable and personal might better be done from a place of trust than a desire to "find out" if there's any point to a relationship—that one undermines the other, in fact.

So recklessly, rather than thoughtfully, she says, "There's more." Taking a few steadying breaths, she rolls back toward him.

This part, she does want to see his face for.

"My work. It's fairly confronting for most people. I'm trained as a lawyer, but I left law a long time ago. Now I do something else. Something that makes me happy and suits my life and is a good choice, not a bad choice, even though most people try to tell me otherwise. But it can be upsetting for people, and I'm prepared for the possibility that you may not wish to continue seeing me after learning this. So before I say it, I want to say that I understand that. And that I'm happy to answer any questions, for as long as it takes.

"So...I'm an escort. I've been doing it for years. And I want you to know that to me, it's just a job—"

Natalie is watching Griffin closely. What passes across a person's face in that first second is usually more telling than what they say in the minutes or days afterwards. She's seen disgust, contempt, even rage. She's also seen compassion, condescension —invariably followed by some kind of "savior" monologue.

She doesn't want to see any of these things on Griffin's face right now. Not if their relationship is to have any hope of surviving at all.

To his credit, she doesn't see anything of this nature. What she does see is a stabbing flash of pain. And before she even knows what is happening he has rolled out of her bed, grabbed his bundle of clothes, and headed for the door.

40

"I HAVE BAD NEWS."

Still reeling from Griffin's wordless departure, Natalie doesn't think she wants to hear what the detective has to say.

She can't believe she could lie there, crying about their lost baby, and he could still react so badly to her being an escort that it didn't even warrant words.

The pain she feels at his leaving her is so intense she can barely answer the detective.

This is why trusting people is utter bullshit, she thinks to herself.

"I went back over the phone records from the earlier murders." Detective Casey doesn't wait for an answer anyway. "That number you gave me for your boyfriend. It was used to contact one of the deceased escorts. The third one to be killed. Not close to her death. But still—I'd like to have a chat with this Griffin. Do you know where I can find him?"

* * *

The rest of the day passes in a blur.

After telling Detective Casey where Griffin usually stayed

when in Sydney, she hung up and contemplated whether it felt worse that, despite her certainty that he is not, the police are now considering her boyfriend a person of interest relating to serial killings of WOC escorts, or that her boyfriend seemed to think she didn't even warrant a single word after sharing two sensitive and hugely vulnerable things with him.

Boyfriend! Oh God. Natalie startles at how easily the title slipped in to her thoughts.

So much for opening herself up to love.

Maybe I'm not built for love, she thinks to herself, the familiar emptiness closing in around her.

She doesn't cry.

She doesn't despair.

She just lies down, and feels very, very tired.

* * *

Hours later, Natalie wakes up from a nap, groggy and confused.

It's the most ridiculous dichotomy—either her boyfriend is a police suspect, or he's just frigging wonderful but has rejected her on the very grounds she always used as a reason to avoid relationships herself.

But through the haze, one thing is abundantly clear to her.

She doesn't wish she wasn't an escort.

She doesn't regret a single day of her career.

In fact, if anything she's proud of it. Not just that she sees people who would otherwise never know intimacy—clients with physical disabilities, intellectual disabilities, crucifying shyness. She rejects wholeheartedly the idea that that's "good" sex work as opposed to "bad" sex work, such as seeing married men or younger men or old men or even fucking irritating, unpleasant, conservative men, who can manage to insult her work choices even as they avail themselves of her services.

Maybe it's her avoidance of intimate relationships and connections that make it seem so normal, but she just doesn't see what all the fuss is about. It's just a job. A well-paid job, an emotionally and physically labor-intensive job, frankly a terribly boring, repetitive job, most of the time.

She wonders if it would be so terrible if her parents knew. It's not like they were a well of support and acceptance anyway. Perhaps what mattered was less their response, and more how she approached things. Perhaps if they were going to reject her anyway, she could learn to speak her truth, regardless of the outcome?

Noting that she's possibly delirious, having not eaten anything at all, all day and having been battered by all the emotional turmoil she usually avoids, she nevertheless feels strangely light and hopeful.

Opening up to Griffin has made her realize a few things. Mainly, that even though he left, she's still okay. She's hurting, and confused, and scared—but somehow, it's opened up the possibility of a new way of being in the world.

She scoops up her keys, and heads down to her car.

It's only later that she realizes she forgot her wallet—and more importantly, her phone.

41

NATALIE ARRIVES AT HER PARENTS' house unannounced.

She doesn't so much as glance at number seven on her way past. Grant Boyd has been forgotten amidst more pressing worries.

The curtain in the living room of his house flickers briefly as she pulls into her parents' driveway, but Natalie doesn't notice.

She doesn't notice the figure standing behind it, looking out.

She's focused on one thing only. Carried on by the fury and the energy of the desperately wounded, she careens into her parents' living room, determined to either demand all their love and acceptance and support *right this minute,* or relinquish it forever.

Upeksha looks up from the couch, startled. Unbridled hostility or demands are not how things are attended to in her house. And Natalie has clearly got all her weapons drawn. Rather than the travel allowing them to dissipate, she's ruminated the whole drive there, her feelings of anger only growing.

"Grant is an arsehole," she howls, fists clenched, teeth grinding as soon as they meet again after the first angry words escape her lips. "You never stood up for us! You never fought for us! People treated us like shit. No one else was brown. No one wanted us to be brown! Not even you."

Ravi has glided into the room, his small frame and trim figure not making a sound on the carpet as he approaches.

"That's enough, Natalie," he says quietly. "You're upset. Go home."

"Yes! I'm upset! You're supposed to comfort me! Support me! Something! Not push me away because you don't want to feel anything yourself. It's your job! You've always opted out of it! Like you signed up for only half the parenting responsibilities. Keep them alive! That's all you bothered with. Not help them feel loved!"

On some level, she knows this approach will not achieve even close to her aims—confrontation means uncertain outcomes, and uncertain outcomes feel risky to her parents. But she can't help herself. It's all suddenly too much. Letitia. Grant. Racism. Griffin. She wants to blame someone who she can have some impact on.

Oddly, it's not suspicion around Griffin and his burner phone and nonexistence that frightens or hurts her. Though she wouldn't admit it, she thinks she's smarter than anyone who might try to play her, and doesn't genuinely feel that Griffin is a threat. A combination of trusting her judgement and an "it won't happen to me" mentality guides her on that front.

No, what stings is his defection following her showing him something of herself, being vulnerable. Even while she can see that the pain is survivable, and that she stands by her choices in a way she's never really been forced to before—by someone outright rejecting them—she's still angry with him for responding this way. She feels almost like she *could* be devastated, and he didn't know that she *wouldn't* be devastated, so his behavior is hurtful and awful and unforgivable.

To not even *speak*.

Coupled with the resentment that has been eating away at

her about her parents for forever means that they are the perfect target to vent all her rage upon.

"I will *not* go home!" she screams, whirling on her father, a finger stabbing at the air. But just as quickly as it came on, the fire goes out of her. Her shoulders slump, her pointing finger dangling uncertainly for a moment, then falling to her side.

"I'm an escort," she says quietly, looking first her mother, then her father in the eyes. "Letitia was an escort. That's how we met. And someone is killing brown escorts. Five so far. The police are even interviewing my boyfriend. So you see? You can't pretend I'm not brown. You can't pretend I'm not part of this. And don't you dare tell me the solution is to change myself. Make my world smaller. Give up my job. I like my job and no racist, murderous arsehole is going to take it away from me. I'll skin him alive if he so much as tries."

With this—pulling herself up to her full height—she gives her parents one last defiant glare before sweeping back out the front door, her visit a whirlwind in every sense of the phrase.

She spun in, she spun out.

At high speed, at high volume.

And left devastation in her wake.

Ravi and Upeksha stare after her in silent shock.

* * *

Post-confession, Natalie drives around in some kind of stunned disbelief.

It doesn't occur to her that "coming out" to her parents, as a truly proud thing to do, might have worked better if she'd stayed to answer questions and convey her pride in her work and her community. Leaving with a giant cymbal crash could be read as defiance, or it could be read as shame.

But she doesn't think about these things. To Natalie, all that matters is that she has spoken some kind of truth to her parents, who are not—and have never been—receptive to it. Maybe it marks a turning point of some kind in their relationship. Or maybe it's meaningless on that front. But she's done *something*. Something on her terms.

She feels both bad and good.

Hopeful and crushed.

Restored and ruined.

It's hard to change the dance you do with your folks, no matter how hard you try.

* * *

It's late by the time she heads home.

If you asked her, she wouldn't have been able to tell you where she went or what she did. Whether someone followed her, or no one did.

If anyone had questioned her about how she felt—driving around with a killer hunting escorts of color, with a boyfriend under suspicion, and without her phone—all she would have said was *tired*.

She felt very, very, very tired.

She wasn't watching out for any danger at all.

She paid no attention to anything except the blur of family-related memories that clashed and chimed and pushed and pulled her in all sorts of directions.

Left her breathless and shaky.

It's bigger than stating she's an escort, and bigger than at last—decades later—telling them how she felt as a brown child, then a brown adolescent in their world.

It's stepping out of line. It's doing what is right for her. It's exhilarating, and terrifying. Because once you take that leap, the dance changes.

And sometimes your partner no longer wants to dance with you at all.

42

BACK IN LINFIELD, Ravi and Upeksha glance at each other.

No words pass between them; none need to. Ravi can see what his wife is thinking by the set of her jaw.

She, too, knows what he is thinking, without even having to look at him.

Nevertheless, she gives him a sidelong glance, to see if he knows that she knows that he knows.

He is looking at her intently, but remains calm and poised.

"Leave it," he says softly. "You promised."

But he knows it's no good.

He's seen that look in her eyes before.

43

THE PLAN HAS BEEN SET *in motion.*

The man hates these fucking "high class" whores, who charge ridiculous amounts of money. Like their pussy is any better than the next one.

He likes to toy with them before he kills them.

He likes to get them panting for his dough.

He pretends to be such a model client. He'll screen without question. He'll offer a deposit. They'll trot along to the booking thinking he's "easy money." A respectful client who knows how it all works and follows the rules.

He makes them pay for it later, though.

Oh yes.

They've all paid the price for their slovenly ways.

Now, he confirms the date and sends a picture of someone else's license.

He pays a cash deposit at an ATM.

Then he waits. Patiently.

Now, it's just a matter of time.

44

BY THE TIME Natalie turns onto her street, she's beyond exhausted.

The day has taken so many turns in unexpected directions that she suddenly, desperately just wants to lie down.

She pulls over opposite the garage door into the apartment car park and hesitates. There's nothing in her fridge. Not even a bottle of wine to lament her day with.

If ever there was a day for take away, this would be it.

Slumping over the steering wheel, suddenly too tired to even hold her head up, she deliberates with closed eyes about whether she is even capable of driving any further. Perhaps delivery or even toast will do for dinner. She's almost certain there's at least some bread in the freezer.

But even as she decides that toast will do, and she can put the car away for the night, there's a sharp rap on her passenger window, then the large shape of a man slides alongside her into her car.

45

THIRTY-YEAR-OLD UPEKSHA COOMMARASWAMY sits back on her heels, the stench of vomit strong in her nostrils.

Her stomach is churning.

Reports of widespread rioting throughout her homeland fill her with terror. Her fears, stirring uneasily inside her ever since the formation of the Liberation Tigers of Tamil Eelam the year prior, have proven well-founded.

Initially, she had felt guilty for her lack of enthusiastic support. Her father had believed passionately in the future of a Tamil state. So much so that he had lost his life, protesting peacefully following the implementation of the Sinhala Only Act in 1956. Upeksha had only been nine at the time.

For a while, in her youth, she was passionately and fervently interested in politics, partly as a way to stay connected to her father, and feel like he was proud of her.

But now she feels dread, not hope.

After trying for three years, she is finally pregnant.

Her eldest brother did not return from work four days ago, and they do not know where he is.

They keep getting reports on various acquaintances who have

not been heard from since the riots started in Jaffna two weeks ago.

What sort of future can she hope for, for the small life growing inside her, in these circumstances?

Ravi is sitting on the edge of the bath next to her, one hand lightly on her back. He should be at work, but he has been unable to find any since being laid off earlier that year, ostensibly due to poor performance, despite being the most diligent and respected professor at the university.

They don't need to speak; both understand that it is not just the new life growing inside Upeksha that is making her nauseous. Reports of acts of violence have given life, dimensions, color to all their fears.

Both Ravi and Upeksha are past wanting to support their people. They want no part in civil war.

They just want somewhere safe to raise their baby.

46

NATALIE SCREAMS.

The man looks surprised, and slightly irritated.

After a few beats, Natalie recognizes Detective Burns from that first day at her parents' house.

She can hear her heavy breathing, feel her heart thudding. Some detached part of her mind is interested to note that she didn't endeavor to flee when presented with danger. Just stared at the intruder in shock.

"I'm sorry," he says, defensive. "I left you a message telling you I was waiting out front."

"Jesus," Natalie mutters. "There's someone killing escorts of color and you just jump into my car without warning?"

Relief is coursing through her, but also frustration that anyone could have so little empathy or insight into the power that they hold. That they just don't think about how terrifying their actions could be.

Natalie frowns, not able to remember when she last saw her phone.

"Anyway," the detective continues, as though terrifying someone could be brushed off after twenty-odd seconds and the conversation continue as normal. "I've been in touch with Detective Casey. She hasn't been able to locate Griffin or get him on the phone. I was going to have a chat with you about Grant Boyd, so I thought I'd drop by to see if he was with you at the same time."

Though Natalie's first thought is why he didn't just call on both accounts, she's too interested in what he has discovered about Grant to ask him. "And?" is all she says, her breathing slowly normalizing.

"We questioned him about Letitia, as you suggested. He wasn't very cooperative. I think you probably summed him up nicely, actually. But Casey's filled me in on the other cases. And he has an alibi for three of them. Mostly, he's been behind bars. So if we are looking for a serial killer—and we believe that we are —he's not our man."

Natalie slumps back in her seat. She didn't know what she expected, but it wasn't that. Surely a phone call would have sufficed for that information to be passed on to her?

She wonders, then, if his visit is to check up on her. To ensure that she is okay, is her first generous thought, and she softens slightly. But then she thinks perhaps it's more likely he's checking that she's not hiding Griffin—far less charitable, she knows, and slightly nonsensical.

Usually, she might try to find out more. But she's simply too tired to even talk.

Her question is answered anyway though. Burns is watching her carefully.

"However, we have gone back over all the descriptions provided by witnesses of people seen in the areas around where each victim was found. It's not a lot to go on, as there aren't really any defining features...but a couple of people saw someone matching Griffin's description in the area of two of the cases. One of them, actually, was your mother. We'd like a photo, if you have one, to take back to these witnesses and see if they recognize him."

Natalie blinks and shakes her head.

"No," she says, and Burns frowns.

"I mean, it's not him. I'm sure of that. But yes, I'll text you a photo. I don't have many." She feels confused and irritated. "But why would he invest months in dating someone? He'd be the first suspect now if I went missing. It doesn't make any sense. You're on the wrong track."

Her irritation growing, Natalie explains that she'll text him later; she doesn't have her phone. Then nods slightly toward the car park, indicating that that's where she's going, and that he's dismissed.

Burns hesitates slightly, then exits the car.

47

ON MONDAY MORNING, Natalie feels as though a truck has not only run over her, but has paused atop her bones for a while, crushing the life right out of her. Then reversed backward and forward a few times for good measure.

She's left several messages for Detective Casey, but can't get through and hasn't heard back.

Not that Griffin has been trying to contact her anyway.

Cup of tea in hand, Natalie slouches back to bed. She's supposed to be seeing a new client at 11 a.m. Ordinarily, feeling like this, she'd just cancel the booking. But the client has paid a deposit which she doesn't want to refund, so she thinks she might as well just get it over with.

Also, she's worked so little of late, she could really use the cash. Her savings has depleted more in the last three months than in the prior three years.

Still, perhaps just a little more sleep, she thinks, crawling back into bed.

She's asleep in about twenty seconds.

* * *

Natalie arrives at the hotel after significant effort.

She really can't be bothered today.

Her parents haven't spoken to her since she stormed out of their house. Not that she expected a follow-up call. More likely, she had expected that they would pretend it never happened. So she *is* surprised to get a text message—for the first time in living memory, cancelling Sunday lunch. *Your mother is unwell,* Ravi had texted, no curter than usual, but the accusation hanging in the ever-present unsaid stuff between them. *Sunday lunch is cancelled.*

Natalie resisted the urge to suggest that perhaps she would have six days to recover between now and Sunday lunch. But she knows what message they want her to understand, and it's quicker just to understand it than to pick it full of holes.

In a way, she's glad she didn't cancel the client. Continuing with work feels like an act of resistance. A rebuttal of their rejection. Dismissal of their protest.

But in another way it feels too hard, with all the unfinished business hanging over her.

Sighing, Natalie steps out of the lift.

She checks her phone.

Brody.

His driver's license is in his text, albeit with a thumb over the photo and address.

A unicorn, maybe?

She snaps her phone shut, and knocks on the door.

48

Brody sits on the bed, *waiting.*

Today will likely bore him.

He needs to be "good." Kind, respectful, easy to please.

Sluts like Ivy don't deserve "good."

Still, good things come to those who wait. This is all just due diligence, to make sure everything goes smoothly for the second "date."

The trick is to be a model client this first time.

Leave it a few weeks.

Then strike.

That's when the real fun begins.

Today: it's just a formality.

He hopes to get it over with as quickly as he can without seeming odd.

49

WHEN THE DOOR opens following her knock, Natalie steps back in shock.

Something deep and primal and terrible kicks in, in a way that it simply didn't in the car with Detective Burns.

She has no time to think: adrenaline surges in her system and she turns and bolts as fast as her Loubs will allow her, before she even realizes that's what she's chosen to do.

Back at the lift, another couple look at her in surprise.

Her eyes dart around frantically as she waits, her limbs twitching, her heart hammering. If they speak to her, she doesn't hear.

When the lift dings, she slips in with them, keeping close, like a shadow.

The client hasn't followed her.

But the panic does. She runs out the revolving doors, her heart thrashing in her chest.

And runs straight into her mother.

50

THIRTY-TWO-YEAR-OLD KANDIAH COOMMARASWAMY wakes up in excruciating pain.

It takes him some time to work out what is happening.

He remembers that he was walking home from work.

He works as an electrician and runs his own business. He loves his work. He loves being able to find a problem and fix it— the orderly nature of it. The way that every problem has a story that he can find and fix.

His skills are renowned around Colombo.

Over the past few weeks—since the riots had broken out— the Sinhalese government had started forcing him to work on army premises. The Tamil Tigers accused him of betraying his people. They threatened to kill him if he didn't stop helping the army.

The army threatened to kill him if he *did* stop helping them.

He has spent the last week in hushed conversations with his family. They all know that whoever follows through on these threats is unlikely to stop at him. If he is in danger, so is his family.

Upeksha and Ravi, Kandiah and his family, Shehara and her

family, and their mother are preparing to leave. They have paid so much money. False documents and a quick exit are not cheap. And though Ravi could show the appropriate qualifications and skills to secure permanent residency as a skilled migrant, they don't have enough time. They need to leave *now*.

All this is irrelevant now, though, as Kandiah slowly comes to understand that his hands have been nailed to a road. He has been told of such stories, but never believed they were true. That the Sinhalese army use a railroad spike on dark mountain roads, leaving their victims the choice of tearing their hands off the road or being crushed by trucks that cannot see them in the dark.

How could it be true, because who would do such a thing to another human being?

Now, in the dark, he can hear laughter in the bushes, as the soldiers take bets on which he will choose.

51

NATALIE AND UPEKSHA stare at each other, both equally alarmed.

Upeksha casts a quick glance over Natalie's person, then takes her elbow and directs her firmly down the street.

"My car is just down here," she says, her voice low, her grip fierce.

She doesn't let go of Natalie's elbow until she has shunted her into the passenger seat, after which she slams the door shut. She walks briskly to the driver's side and gets in, locking the car after her, businesslike and efficient.

Natalie continues to stare at her. Her heart is still pounding erratically, her breathing heavy. She can't think. She can't even put her seatbelt on. Upeksha reaches across her, buckling her in in one smooth motion, then starting the engine.

Without waiting for information or instructions, she starts driving toward Natalie's flat.

* * *

After ten minutes of silence, Natalie's brain starts to function again.

"Why are you here?" she asks, her voice uncertain. She means at the hotel, even though the very fact that they're driving away from it is what has allowed the adrenaline to subside and the sense of imminent danger and the panic to pass.

"What happened?" Upeksha shoots back, her voice calm but firm.

Natalie just shrugs and stares out the window. As her system struggles to process the surge of adrenaline, she feels washed out. Astonishingly, she feels like crying. Again.

With Upeksha, that would absolutely never do.

With some effort, Natalie tries to focus.

Trying to claw back her way to herself, she kicks off her shoes and throws them into the backseat, along with her wig. She's trying to emit defiance, but she's shaking, and her mother can see it, despite her bravado. But she can't yet make sense of what has just happened, let alone find words to try to share it with the one person who doesn't like to be shared with. Who never wants to know.

Not without collapsing in a howling mess.

Natalie fights against her tears fiercely. It feels like self-protection—like life and death, almost. She doesn't understand it, but vulnerability with Upeksha has never felt like a safe place. Her response is automatic.

"What happened?" Upeksha repeats, her voice harder this time. Steely, almost. "Something's wrong. Don't pretend. A mother knows."

Natalie capitulates.

Later, she would think back over the conversation and feel confused by how much she shared. She might even laugh: an ugly, bitter laugh. *Did you know all through my childhood?* she might think to herself. *What about through high school? What about through life?*

But now, frightened and confused, she answers Upeksha's questions.

"I don't know," she says. "I had a client there. I didn't stay. That client...he looked..." Her words dry up, fade out. She can't make sense of what is happening.

Because that client? He looked just like her boyfriend.

* * *

Disarmed by Upeksha's sudden appearance of "wanting to know," Natalie tells her all of it.

About Griffin not existing. About his phone being linked to a dead escort. And about her fleeing her booking just now because the client looked just like Griffin.

About her fear that she might be going mad.

You never give up hope entirely, it seems. Connection to her mother seems worth trying for, still. After all these years.

When her guard is down. When she feels vulnerable.

She's not capable of thinking clearly. But when she mulls over it later, unsettled, it seems to her that some primal part of her still moved her toward connecting, still seemed to think it worth the risk. Still thought it was possible. It seemed right there, so close Natalie could feel her longing more strongly than she had felt it in thirty years.

Maybe this time, her whole being seemed to be screaming at her. Trying to catapult her into her mother's arms, and some imagined blissful comfort she might find there. Being taken care of by her mother.

But Upeksha is businesslike. She asks for some details, and to see a photo of Griffin. Natalie only has a couple of poorly executed selfies, the same ones she sent to Burns. She has no idea why her mother needs to see a picture. But she feels too overwhelmed to resist or try to figure it out.

Upeksha drops her at home without reassurances, without looking after her, and without even touching her.

She does tell her matter-of-factly to stop seeing strange men in unknown places as she drives away.

52

BEFORE SHE HAS EVEN SET her bag down, let alone has time to process what just happened, there's demanding knocking at her door.

Natalie freezes.

Did someone just watch her come home?

But Griffin's manly voice carries through the door.

"Babe, are you there? We need to talk."

Yes. We do, thinks Natalie. But she can't think clearly.

Brown escorts are being murdered.

Your phone can be linked to them.

A man who looked like you just booked a date with me.

"Hon?"

For some reason, the endearment grates on Natalie. While she's wondering about being attacked and murdered, Griffin gets to play happy partners. It all seems ludicrous and unfair.

Sliding down the door, Natalie sits on the floor and calls him on her mobile.

"Hon?" he says again, this time into his phone. "What's going on? Can I come in?"

"No," says Natalie. At least this is one sensible decision she can make. "Let's talk like this."

"Oh." Griffin is silent for a moment. "Is something wrong? I mean I know I left. It's unforgivable. I want to say sorry. In person. To your face."

"Did Detective Casey get in touch with you?"

Silence.

The space drags on between them.

Natalie doesn't know exactly what to ask, so she doesn't ask anything.

"Yes. It's not what you think," he says, rushed, suddenly. "There's some things I need to tell you. About...escorts. My past."

"Jesus Christ. Please tell me you haven't murdered anybody."

"Ivy! Jesus! How can you ask me that?"

"Gosh. I don't know. You don't legally seem to exist in Australia and you haven't volunteered your real name. Your phone has been linked to dead women. And I just had someone try to book me who bore a remarkable resemblance to you. What the fuck am I supposed to think? What would you think if you were in my shoes? Cause Jesus. Fuck. To be honest, I can't even comprehend this mess let alone come up with a coherent response to it. All I know is something is wrong and you're at the center of it. I'd like to keep a locked door between us for a while."

More silence on the other side of the door.

Then: "Ivy. This client. *What did he say his name was?*"

Natalie wipes tears angrily from her eyes. She feels overwhelmed and hurt and worried and confused.

What was her mother even doing at that hotel?

The word drops into her mind out of nowhere.

Longing.

What's she's feeling is longing, she realizes. Longing for everything to be normal, and for Griffin to just be her sexy boyfriend, and for being open with people not to cause so much grief, so much chaos.

Then Griffin, more urgently, leaning against the solid door between them: "*Ivy! This client! What was his name?!*"

"Brody," Natalie sniffles, defeated. She feels so tired.

She just wants to lie down. Right there, in front of the door.

Lie down, and close her eyes, and never have to worry about any of this ever, ever again.

It's like her body is mutinying, just when she needs to work everything out. Just when she needs to be alert and on guard. Mentally agile.

Is this a form of resistance? she wonders, her thoughts sluggish. *Opting out?*

She slides down a little further. She lets her eyes droop.

Right now, she's safe. She could just rest for ten minutes. Just five, even.

Is this what being emotional looks like? she wonders. *All your purpose and energy diverted into something so pointless and obscure?*

She wishes she'd never laid eyes on Griffin. Her life was going along just fine before him.

But just as she is agreeing with herself that, yes, it would be ok just to close her eyes for a minute or two, just to rest for the barest of minutes, she hears a resounding click.

And feels the door push in against her with more force than she is ready to push back against in her lethargic, dispirited state.

53

THE MAN WALKS out of the hotel, agitated.

He paces outside for several minutes, frowning and cursing.

He is sure that Ivy could not have recognized him. He doesn't know what just happened.

He's angry that his plan has been derailed at the first act.

In his mind, he goes back over every time he has seen Ivy. There's not one glance in his direction, not a flash of suspicion in any of his memories.

He doesn't take well to his plans being upended.

Impulsively, he goes back to his room. He's got cash; he's got a nice hotel room for the night. Though he works a mediocre job and hasn't had a promotion in ten years, he is excellent at living cheaply so he can splurge when it suits him.

He's damn well going to make some use of it.

He books the cheapest girls he can find, all four of them.

He's already splurged far too much on the lush room, to convey to Ivy that he is the ideal client—rich as well as kind.

Some shitty cheap white girls can at least suck his dick while he works out what to do next.

54

KANDIAH DOES NOT REMEMBER MAKING a decision.

Perhaps, with the sound of the trucks approaching in the darkness, a bodily instinct to survive took over conscious thought.

Somehow, he finds his way home. Which is surprising, as his mind is not functioning. He cannot remember any part of the journey, or how long it took.

His mother has been killed, and is nailed to the wall in the kitchen.

The rest of his family are nowhere to be seen.

In the living area, Ravi's family lie scattered amidst pools of sticky, half-dried blood. His two younger sisters. His mother and father. Kandiah remembers they were coming on the day the families were to leave.

Kandiah does not know what day it is. He does not know how long he was held by the Sinhalese army, or how long he was on the road before he came to. But he has nothing else to do but to head to the place the families had agreed to meet to leave Sri Lanka. They were to be smuggled by boat to India while they wait for their false documents to be processed, so they can all move to Australia.

Before he leaves, Kandiah tries to get his mother down from the wall, but his fingers are too mangled.

He tries and tries, to give her this one last dignity. But eventually, he has to give up.

Crying silently, he stumbles out into the night.

55

IT TAKES a few moments for Natalie's brain to catch up with what her body is detecting.

Griffin, in her flat. Somehow. *Breaking* into her flat.

Despite her exhaustion, she scrabbles away from the door, but her body feels heavy and sluggish. She makes a lunge toward the kitchen—*knives,* she's thinking—but Griffin is already above her.

Fuck it, she thinks, feeling the heat from his body. *Maybe death is better than this fucking nonsense anyway.* She huddles in a ball at his feet, barely daring to look at him. But Griffin is leaning over her, concern and some degree of panic in his eyes.

"*Brody?*" he's asking her, searching her eyes. "*BRODY?*"

Confused, Natalie at last pulls herself up to sitting, Griffin holding her elbow almost tenderly.

"You know him?" she asks. "You're related?"

Griffin shakes his head.

"Brody is *me.* That's *my* real name." He searches her eyes for a moment, hesitating. Then: "I think you might have met my brother."

"You never mentioned a brother," Natalie says, frowning. "Only a sister."

"It's complicated. I'll explain later. We need to—"

"*No. Now*," Natalie says, leaning away from him, feeling like she might vomit again. *What were the chances of your partner's brother booking you? Like, a million to one? Or, not an issue for people in* normal *relationships where your partner gives you their fucking real name, so you might recognize a family member before accepting the booking?*

The irony of Griffin still calling her Ivy has escaped her, though, to be fair, she had attempted to explain it.

"We should call that detective," Griffin pleads, grabbing Natalie's hands. "I promise I'll explain everything. But we should call her now, while he might still be at the hotel."

Natalie hesitates for a second, and then nods. She finds the number in her phone and hits the call button, handing it to Griffin. She doesn't even know what she's meant to tell Casey.

Griffin puts the phone to his ear. "What's the room and hotel?" he asks Natalie, concentrating, focused. He looks handsome and in control, despite his urgency. Natalie realizes that she is trusting him, without even making a clear decision to do so. But she goes—like so many times before—with her gut.

"Oh shit. It's in my phone." She gestures for him to give it back, but he holds a hand up. A moment later, he leaves a rushed message for the detective, asking her to call him urgently, that his brother is using his name and may still be a hotel in the CBD. Then he gives Natalie back the phone to find the room number.

Once she relays it to him, they stare at each other.

"From the start," Natalie says. She is watching him warily, but in that three minutes, something has changed. She couldn't articulate what it was—the concern in his eyes as he helped her to sit up? His tenderness toward her, even as he takes control of the situation so efficiently and decisively?—but she knows, without a doubt, that her physical safety is not at risk from this man. She believed it before, but she trusts it absolutely now.

She takes a deep breath, and waits.

56

WHEN THE KNOCK comes on the door, three of the working girls are still servicing the man.

Massaging his shoulders, stroking his ego, performing in front of him. He sends one of them to answer the door, thinking it's the fourth girl coming back, now ready to perform natural oral, which she initially refused and he'd kicked her out, snatching his money back and towering over her threateningly.

But the woman accompanying Alice or Annie, or whatever her name is, back into the room is older.

Browner.

Andrew's lips curl in distaste.

But she waves a wad of fifty-dollar notes around and smiles at him, composed and confident, like she knows what needs to happen and somehow making the man feel calmer, less erratic.

"I'll pay you to send these girls away," she says. "I have a proposition for you."

"I don't want to fuck your dirty old brown cunt," he sneers back, but he reaches for the money, and the other girls scurry out of the room.

"Leave some lingerie," the woman tells them curtly. "Consider it my payment for your early mark."

"You're not going to fit your fat arse into their clothes, grandma," Andrew taunts her, but his dick is getting hard again thinking about what he might be able to make her do. To humiliate her.

She just smiles politely.

"Let me finish that shoulder rub," she says, kicking off her shoes.

"Are you a fancy whore, too?" Andrew asks, eyeing the red soles. He's looked at enough adverts to know which shoes the pricey girls wear.

Still, he doesn't protest as she walks behind him, her head held high, graceful in her movements. He's done a few lines, and can't bring himself to give two fucks about basically anything. She can pay him to rub his shoulders if she wants to, the silly cunt.

She places one hand lightly on his shoulder, and hands him some expensive champagne, purchased on the way. She makes sure to flash the label at him, knowing instinctively that men like this don't refuse drugs or booze. Then she massages his shoulders firmly and confidently as he sips at it, emanating a calm peacefulness, which he enjoys, despite himself.

He doesn't notice the cheap, functional handbag slung over her shoulder, at odds with her glamourous hair and shoes, the champagne, her stately demeanor.

Inside it, all she carries are a knife, some unlabeled tablets, and a few plastic bags.

57

IT'S A MIRACLE, but they are all there.

Huddled in the dark, with only the clothes on their backs, they are hustled onto a boat in the dark. They have spent their combined life savings to be smuggled to India while they await falsified documents to travel on to Australia.

They have been told that a place has been arranged for them to stay at until the documents arrive.

It turns out to be some sheets of corrugated roofing strung up in a corner of a street.

They have no money, no contacts, no support.

They don't speak of what they left behind.

They wait for the smugglers to return.

They never do.

58

SETTLED on the floor opposite Natalie, Griffin takes a deep breath.

"When my mum left my dad, my brother was helping him fix the tractor, and he refused to come with us to school. Mum was never allowed to drive the ute, but my father had broken my nose. Mum used it as an excuse to drive into town, to take me to the doctor. But she left the ute near the doctor's and got us on a train. We went to Sydney and never went back."

Griffin is silent for a while.

"I can't imagine my brother had a very nice time with my father. When Brian—that's my father—realized she'd left him, he would have taken it out on the nearest thing weaker than him. And I can't imagine how Andrew must have felt, being left behind. I do know how much it hurt my mother. I found her crying nearly every day for months."

Natalie is staring at Griffin, shocked.

It's a whole other world of family pain that she can't even begin to wrap her head around.

"Mum saved money and paid someone to go and get him, but it took ages. She was too scared to go anywhere near Dad herself.

So he was there with Dad, just the two of them, for maybe two or three years. He was a very angry boy by the time he came to live with us. But he came. He stayed. Mum bent over backwards trying to make it right. But of course, she couldn't. How could you? That's a long time to feel abandoned. No matter what she said to him, she left him behind and it meant he was different to us. He'd experienced horrors we didn't want to even try to imagine."

Griffin pauses for a long time. The air grows heavy between them.

"What then?" Natalie whispers eventually. There's something else, she can feel it. Rolling and boiling like a rebel wave that's going to dump you so badly you'll be shitting sand for weeks.

Griffin clears his throat.

"We had no money. Mum hadn't worked barely ever, and only on the farm since she'd married Brian. So that's why..." he looks at her pleadingly, but she doesn't get it. "I'm so sorry I walked out on you after you told me about escorting. My mother worked in a brothel. That's how we survived. But she also died working. And it was just too much. I just needed some air. I didn't want to...I couldn't..." And then he sobs, a wracking, painful, inhuman noise. But as Natalie moves toward him, to comfort him, a golf ball in her throat, her phone rings.

"Detective Casey," she answers, her voice anguished. One hand on Griffin's knee.

She gives the detective the hotel and room number where she met "Brody," but she still doesn't quite know why. "He's using Griffin's real name. And driver's license, I think," she tells her, but shakes her head at Griffin in confusion. But all Detective Casey says is "I'll be in touch," leaving the phone beeping in her ear.

"Why are you worried about Andrew?" Natalie asks, confused. "You think he's dangerous?"

"He gave me this phone. Said he'd got a new, better one, and I might as well use it while I saw to getting mine repaired. I'd just told him I'd dropped mine in the loo. They couldn't fix mine, and I've just kept using it. I keep meaning to get a new Smartphone, but it's never really been a priority. So he had the phone when the other escort was called. It's not much, but Detective Casey wanted to follow it up. And—"

Griffin stops, frowns. A look of agony crosses his face.

"And he hates sex workers," he says softly, finally, his face anguished. "He abused Mum about it until the day she died."

59

AFTER NATALIE STORMED out of their lounge room that day, Upeksha thought, once again, about survival.

She had thought a lot about survival, for a while.

What one might do to preserve life.

She and Ravi fled, changed their names, and cut all ties to their homeland. To preserve life.

Kandiah tore his hands off the road and walked several miles, blood dripping from his mangled fingers, his mind unable to compute the level of horror he had experienced. To preserve life.

The Tamil Tigers strapped bombs to themselves to take out high-profile targets. Others fought with cyanide capsules around their necks.

To preserve a way of life, perhaps.

There were other things they did, to preserve life.

She and Ravi never talk about them.

When new "helpers" came, to their slum shelter on the streets of India, Upeksha had no doubt that they were part of the same group of "helpers" who had abandoned them there. Who else would have known where to find them and what they needed?

Another helper offering salvation—for the right price.

When they'd said they had no money, he'd looked slyly at Upeksha. The youngest, the prettiest of the group.

"She could work for us, for a few weeks," he'd said, leering. "While you wait for the documents to be prepared."

They didn't have any other options. He'd said it would cover food for the family as well, and proper lodgings. Upeksha had agreed. Terrified for her baby. Shehara had tried to take her place, but the man was adamant. They wanted Upeksha.

The rest of the family couldn't look at her the day she was led away.

That man had been her first client, and an almost daily visitor after that.

He had also been the one who drove them to the airport, seven weeks later. All of them thinner, sicker, and more broken than they were before.

The food and lodgings promised had barely been enough to keep them alive.

Upeksha had waited until the whole family were out of the car.

The driver leered at her in the rear-vision mirror. She had moved to get out of the car, but from under her clothes pulled a large knife that she had stolen from the house they'd kept her family in. Upeksha had only been reunited with them that morning.

She drew the blade across his neck, with all the strength afforded her by helplessness and rage.

It was harder than she had anticipated. She was pregnant, weak, and sick.

It was a stupid thing to do. As soon as she started the motion, she realized that. She suddenly saw all the ways that it could go wrong. The danger that she'd put her family in.

Her baby.

But she had thought about it so often.

She had tested the blade that morning as they ate their mouthfuls of stale bread.

It was easier in her imagination. One quick slice. A silent, painful death.

Stupid. How easily he could have stopped their departure if she had failed to at least incapacitate him. He could have screamed. Someone could have caught them, stopped them from boarding their flight, oh so easily.

But she hadn't thought about that.

All she had thought was that she needed something. Some line in the sand.

Some way of stating her non-acceptance of this method. Of her fate.

Of the fate of all the other women who might come after her.

But he didn't call out or chase them. So she must have hurt him badly enough.

She never knew if she killed him. She tells herself that she did, sometimes, when she wakes with nightmares.

It allows her breathing to settle, and her to get back to sleep.

It allows her to get on with her life.

60

NATALIE AND GRIFFIN are still sitting on the kitchen floor, holding hands, when the detective calls them.

She conveys the news in a matter-of-fact manner. Though she prefaces it with condolences, she is clearly not expecting the news to be upsetting.

They have found a deceased Caucasian male at the hotel room Natalie provided. The license he is carrying is out of date, and shows a picture that Detective Casey believes is indeed Griffin, though the likeness is obvious between the two men.

The name on it says Brody Allen Pierce.

She needs Natalie to go to the station to make a statement.

Later, when the police have finished at the crime scene, she'll need Griffin to go to the morgue to identify the body.

They agree, but stay seated on the floor after the call ends.

Just staring at each other.

61

In his last moments, Andrew was thinking about his mother.

When she first arrived in Sydney, she rented a room from a leery old man in Kings Cross.

Far, far away from Brian and fists and fear, Catelyn had found the work that desperate women always find.

She worked as much as she was able while the children were in school. It was rough work. Dangerous, with few support options. But she worked hard, and she put her kids to bed every night herself.

And she loved them.

She loved them hugely.

Fiercely, protectively.

Guiltily.

She gave them enough love for three children, and a day didn't go by when she didn't feel the third child's absence in her whole body. Like a knife.

When the three of them curled up to sleep together, her joining them in the early hours of the morning—the kids way too old now to all sleep in the same bed, but she couldn't afford anything more than the one bedroom apartment—she missed his small body with a yearning that was like dying a little, all over again, every night.

By the time she tried to tell him this, though, he was no longer a little boy.

His body was no longer small.

Working on the farm full-time—having dropped out of school to help when Catelyn left—resulted in a solid, well-defined physique, which was somehow even more menacing on an eleven-year-old boy.

Living with Brian resulted in a closed-off, hardened, angry soul, which was even more so.

Catelyn tried to reach him, to pull him into their world of softness and laughter, despite the scarcity—she had spent years saving money, to send for him. She paid a trusted colleague cash. She paced endlessly for the entire time she waited.

She was gobsmacked that he came.

Andrew never knew it, but she was terrified that he would be firmly his father's son, and pass their location on to Brian, to come for them and take—or kill—them all.

But she'd also spent years growing strong and resourceful. She had enough back-up plans to sink a small boat.

She tried to reach him with love and light. With her whole heart. Up against three years of guilt and pain and suffering, on both their shoulders.

But he was unreachable, and hovered around the outside of their lives in a darkness and coldness that permeated their tiny flat.

He called her a "whore," like he knew what it meant.

But he stayed with them.

He went back to school.

He was angry. But he was safe, she told herself, every night when she came home and looked at them. Together at last.

She knew he wasn't safe from what was inside him. Entrenched there through what he had endured. But she didn't know how to fix that except with love. Consistent, relentless, enormous love.

She couldn't think about it too deeply. Instinctively, she knew that to delve into that would kill her.

Because she left him.

And he never forgot it.

* * *

The drugs the woman had dissolved in his champagne made Andrew so sleepy, he didn't even notice her slipping a plastic bag over his head.

She's standing behind him where he lounges in the chair, slumped down in it, already starting to slide off it to the floor.

Everything is heavy and strange and slow.

In his mind, he sees Catelyn smiling at him, even as he insulted her.

"I'm so sorry," she's whispering, her long, soft hair tickling his face. "I love you," she's saying, the light dancing in her eyes, and her smile, which never falters.

"I love you I love you I love you."

He's never stopped hating her. Hating women. Hating whores. But in those last moments, as he drifts into unconsciousness, he feels an overwhelming urge to stroke her face. To curl into her arms. To smell her hair.

In death, he might love her more than he ever allowed himself to in life.

62

IN ANDREW'S LAST MOMENTS, Upeksha had been thinking about her mother, too.

Kandiah had spared her the details. He could not speak the details. Not of what happened to their family, or what happened to him. Though they could make a guess, from looking at his hands.

He had never been able to work as an electrician again.

* * *

There was a time in her life when it would have been unthinkable to Upeksha that she was capable of killing somebody.

Even when she started following Natalie—after that day when Natalie declared that someone was killing her colleagues—she hadn't been thinking of killing anybody. Just being there. Being near.

But in truth, Upeksha never stopped thinking about life versus death.

What she might do to protect her family.

What she had done to protect her family.

Not her country—she doesn't understand that concept at all. She would not sacrifice her life for a Tamil state.

But for her family...that was another matter.

The day Alex was hurt, she was too late.

She was too immersed in fear. Of being discovered, and being sent back.

But the war is over now.

And she had not survived this far to let her children die.

She didn't have a plan, or a strategy, or even any conviction that she would be enough.

She hadn't even intended to go back to the hotel until Natalie showed her the photo of Griffin.

She hadn't missed a beat. But upon seeing that picture, her plans changed.

* * *

Though it was clearly a different man, the likeness was undeniable to the man Upeksha had seen near the bus stop the day that Letitia was supposed to come for lunch.

Upeksha had been coming back from the shops. She'd wanted fresh produce to cook Letitia something special. Whatever Natalie thought about her prejudice against skin colors, Upeksha was thrilled to meet her daughter's friend. Letitia seemed just like the sort of friend every woman needed.

Upeksha wanted to embrace her, to adopt her. To make her one of the family.

She had no idea that that would be the last thing that Natalie would appreciate.

Weighed down with fresh produce, Upeksha had carefully exited the bus, lifting her shopping cart down each step painstakingly. She did not want any produce crushed or bruised.

The bus had been late, and Upeksha had cursed, and wished

she had let Ravi drive her. But she enjoyed shopping by herself. The orderliness of everything she needed, in neat rows at her fingertips. The cool shopping centers. The purposefulness of the (mainly women) shoppers.

Now, she was late. The meat was already cooking, but Letitia would be arriving in half an hour. She would barely have time to get the bread and vegetables on before Letitia knocked on the door.

She only noticed the man because he was staring at her over his shoulder, twisting awkwardly, as she carefully descended from the bus, with an expression that unsettled her. It was dislike, certainly, and that was unusual enough around here. Their suburb was middle class and well-behaved. Everybody was friendly, but kept largely to themselves. Open hostility was rare enough these days to stand out.

There was no way a brown teenager would be abused in her street anymore.

But it wasn't even that. It was that he had driven away immediately after, but then she had seen him drive past and stare at her again just a few minutes later, heading directly back to where he had just been.

Upeksha felt uneasy.

So many years had passed.

And since the attack on Alex, nothing untoward had ever happened to her. Nothing with any consequences, that is.

Sure, there were obscenities shouted now and then. She was overlooked or underserviced. But nothing that was going to hurt her.

Nothing that was going to *kill* her.

Nevertheless, Upeksha was still hyper vigilant to the expression on men's faces when they looked at her. Fifteen-hour days in a grimy Indian sex shop, terrified for the life of her baby, had taught her to pick up on those that might want to hurt her versus those that just wanted to have sex.

Not that anticipating violence ever meant that she escaped it. Just that she would try to protect her baby, her stomach area, as best she could.

She had wondered about the man, because she feared he went around the block to shout abuse at her. From the look on his face, she even feared he might assault her. But he drove past, slowing only slightly, and Upeksha's awareness had been laser focused on getting home, or which house she could duck into should he reappear. Which neighbor might be friendly enough to open the door.

* * *

Though she had reported him to the detectives that day they came to her house, she was ashamed to admit she could only describe the danger she sensed from him—not any identifying details about his car that might have helped them to locate him.

But then, driving away from Natalie's apartment, it occurred to Upeksha that she knew where he was.

63

THE INVESTIGATION IS OVER QUICKLY.

Of the four young sex workers the police wanted to talk to, they could only find one. Only one number was listed in Andrew's phone, and she is captured on CCTV leaving the hotel alone, as she'd stated, after refusing to perform natural oral.

She didn't know the other girls, she said in her statement.

They were just on the street when she got the call.

Her story didn't budge, and despite a call for public help with the CCTV footage of the other three girls circulated widely, nobody came forward to identify them.

There were small discrepancies.

The CCTV caught the other three girls leaving the hotel, at a time when the medical examiner declared that Andrew was still alive, based on the time-of-death estimate.

Numerous burner phones were found in Andrew's room in a grimy sharehouse, not far from where he and Griffin had lived with Catelyn and Marilyn. Between those and Griffin's phone, the police could link Andrew to all five murdered escorts within weeks of their deaths. DNA evidence linking him followed soon after.

His death was ruled as a homicide by asphyxiation. There was speculation that he had been drugged prior to asphyxiation—traces of several depressants were found in an empty bottle of champagne—but there were numerous over-the-counter as well as illicit substances found at the scene and in his system, so it wasn't conclusive who was giving them to whom, and with what intent.

Timelines surmised that he had organized an orgy with sex workers immediately after Natalie had left (her hasty exit and distress also caught on CCTV), and had taken numerous substances with them. They left just before midday, and the time of death was estimated to be between midday and 12:30 p.m. The police had arrived at 12:39 p.m.

The means of asphyxiation was not found at the scene.

But they had no leads, and to Natalie's surprise, resources were quickly funnelled elsewhere. The case wasn't officially closed, but it seemed that the death of a white man—who could be considered to have deserved it—wasn't a top priority for the homicide squad.

Andrew sank out of the world without a trace.

64

AT THE TIME Upeksha was running late, and hurrying away from the bus stop and the man that had caused alarm bells to ring throughout her body, she was unaware that Letitia was running early.

Due to the late bus, Letitia's bus had in fact pulled up behind Upeksha's own. The driver had waited for Upeksha to disembark too, to then be able to move into the correct bus zone to open the doors. Letitia was looking at her phone though, working out which way she needed to walk to reach Upeksha and Ravi's house. She didn't look up, and she didn't see Upeksha getting off the bus or hurrying away.

Neither Letitia nor Upeksha knew it, but Andrew had been following Letitia's bus since she boarded it.

His careful plan was about to be executed.

Two weeks earlier, he had booked Letitia at a five-star CBD hotel. He'd been kind, respectful, and had sent her off early with a big tip. All things which he hoped would work in his favor now, as he "ran into" her on the street.

Usually, he propositioned his victims. *He lived just around the*

corner and was just heading home between meetings. Did she have
time for a 15-minute blow n go? He had five-hundred dollars. He lives
by himself; there will be no one else there...

It had worked every time. After all, he had screened without
fuss the previous time. He had been a perfect client. And most
people could spare fifteen minutes for five-hundred dollars...

He drove slowly past her bus, having seen Letitia standing up
to exit.

He pulled in ahead of the buses and craned his neck to check
if Letitia was definitely exiting, not just getting ready for the next
stop, and saw a nondescript old brown woman taking forever to
exit, blocking Letitia's bus.

He shot her a disgusted look, hoping she'd move faster.

Finally, she got off and her bus pulled away. Letitia was
definitely on the steps of her bus, preparing to disembark.

Andrew quickly pulled away. His plan was to drive around the
block, and if necessary the adjacent blocks, until he saw her. He
had to be quick, in case her destination was close by.

Barely two minutes passed before Andrew saw Letitia on the
street, her arms swinging easily as she strode along the path that
Upeksha had trodden just five minutes before.

A few minutes more, and she might have seen Upeksha ahead
of her; called out to her; listened to her lament the late bus and
reassured her that she was in no hurry.

As it was, Andrew pulled up alongside her with a wide grin.

"Fancy seeing you here!" he said, the window whirring as it
lowered.

He was dressed in a business suit and an expensive-looking
tie.

Letitia had hesitated, then moved toward the open window.

Andrew was an attractive man.

She remembered him. She remembered their pleasant tryst.
The large tip.

She smiled back, and he fed her his line.

The sun was shining, and she was early.

She slipped into his car.

Smiled her big smile.

She thought to herself that this day could not get any better.

But then it got worse.

65

TENTATIVELY, Griffin introduces Natalie to his sister.

Marilyn is wary and skittish, until Natalie answers questions about her job honestly. Then, unexpectedly, she starts to cry.

They don't talk about Andrew.

Natalie and Griffin have canvassed that topic enough that Natalie never wants to talk about him again.

Her feelings changed for Griffin at the police station. After making her statement, Griffin was also interviewed. He asked if Natalie could stay in for it. Then he spoke at length about his childhood, and what it was like when Andrew joined him, Marilyn, and Catelyn in Sydney.

He admitted that Brian still lived near the farm where they had lived as children, but stated that he has never been in touch with him, and always refers to him as deceased. "He's dead to me," he says, and shrugs.

He speaks about Andrew's verbal violence toward Catelyn.

Of Catelyn's guilt and unrelenting love. How she tried to make it up to him, but never, ever could.

He spoke about how angry Andrew remained all these years later, whenever he got in touch with Griffin and they had a pint.

"He wasn't a pleasant guy to be around," Griffin said. "But I always felt guilty about him being left behind. Every time, I wanted to try to help him. And every time, I walked away with a bad taste in my mouth."

Andrew was sixteen when Catelyn was killed, in a car accident with a client. Andrew had gloated when she died: *That's what whores get! Exactly what's coming for them.* Griffin had organized for Andrew and Marilyn to go live with Catelyn's sister in Melbourne, but Andrew never turned up. Every couple of years he would get in touch with Griffin, but he never told him where he was living or what he was doing. Griffin always got the sense that he wasn't doing well, but he was never receptive to Griffin's offers of support.

"I would never have thought he would actually hurt anyone, though," Griffin stated, pensive. He squeezes Natalie's hand hard.

"So your mother left him, and he never forgave her. It doesn't sound like he had the resources or insight to work through it," Detective Casey muses. "But why would he target escorts of color, rather than white escorts, like his mother, do you suppose?"

Griffin had looked thoughtful.

Natalie watched him carefully, a painful tightness in her chest.

She stops herself from answering for him.

Waits, breathing deliberately slowly.

In, out. In, out.

Finally, he speaks. "If someone's fucked up enough to want to kill escorts because you're angry with your mother, frankly, I think you're clutching at straws to try to find too much logic in his motives." He pauses, goes to speak and then stops, glancing at Natalie again for a second.

Natalie wills him on. Wills Casey to stay silent.

Keeps very still.

"I suppose, it's maybe about the response?" He glances at her again, his assessment more a question than a confident statement of fact. But he carries on, the answer unpolished, not considered before this moment. But forming, nevertheless.

"I suppose he thought it was easier to get away with it? Even the murder of marginalized women like sex workers might draw too much attention if they're affluent and white?"

* * *

After the frenzy of the investigation dies down, Upeksha drops in on Natalie unannounced.

She lets herself in with the key she insisted Natalie give her years earlier "in case of an emergency."

She makes irrelevant small talk, and wanders around the flat. Natalie's skin bristles: it looks like Upeksha is checking up on her, again. Assessing her standard of living.

Murmuring about inane things as she moves around, Natalie switches off, rolling her eyes at Griffin (now his legal name) behind her mother's back. She stops following Upeksha around the flat, giving up on understanding what she is doing.

Instead, she goes back to what she was doing before she was interrupted: making Griffin a cup of tea.

She can hear Upeksha rustling in her bedroom. But she swallows the rush of rage rising in her body.

More of the same, she thinks to herself determinedly, the phrase somehow comforting. Her mother will never change.

She doesn't see Upeksha calmly and quickly return a long black wig and a pair of Louboutins to the back of her wardrobe.

Months later, she'll discover them there, in a strange spot where she doesn't keep either wigs or shoes, and remember.

Running into her mother outside the hotel when she fled Andrew's room.

Taking them off in the car.

She'll remember the mention of an older brown woman on the CCTV approaching Andrew's room at the hotel, the telltale flash of red visible on her feet, the face hidden behind long black hair. The halfhearted request for her to come forward as a witness, drowned under all the images of the three young sex workers. Even Natalie, usually so tuned in to mentions of race, barely gave it a second thought.

She'll never ask Upeksha about it, and she'll never know for sure.

But Natalie holds onto it. Feels it in her bones as an act of love.

* * *

Now though—she sees Griffin watching her, witnessing her reset herself against her mother's intrusion.

Noticing.

Getting it.

She smiles at him warmly, and hands him his tea.

EPILOGUE

IN RAVI and Upeksha's backyard, Griffin is barbequing steaks and chatting to Eloise.

Natalie can see that Eloise is enjoying herself. Occasionally, she throws her head back and laughs, her smile wide, her teeth perfect. She looks natural and comfortable, but Natalie can see that she is full of wonder at the circumstances.

Griffin looks handsome and relaxed, managing the steaks and being attentive to her friend both important to him, and both things he does with ease.

He looks like he belongs there. Charming everyone at a family barbeque like he'd known them his whole life.

Natalie is sitting with Alex.

She's made a point of coming by every week. She told Alex she wants to see more of him. She asks him more questions. About his work. About how he manages aspects of his life in relation to what he knows about how his brain works. She talks to him more openly, more confidingly. Sometimes, he responds in kind; sometimes, he does not. Sometimes, he drifts off and plays with his figurines.

Upeksha and Ravi are quietly delighted. Their house is filled with laughter more on the days Natalie comes to see Alex. Even on the days he's not receptive to company, Natalie stays with them and chats. To them, she seems less on edge and more accepting than she has her entire life.

When he's in town, Griffin accompanies Natalie, and they approve of his commitment to family time. They suspect, rightly, that Natalie's softening—toward them, toward life in general—has something to do with him. Sometimes, she even brings Eloise, and secretly they hope that Eloise might fall in love with Alex. It's far-fetched, they know that. But they hope for it anyway.

Now, Griffin plates up their steaks, remembering that Ravi likes his blue, and Upeksha likes hers without a hint of blood. He tops up their glasses, and they swoon at his thoughtfulness. While Natalie rolls her eyes at his failure to multi-task, he will always stop what he is doing to really listen, even to them, and they adore him.

Everyone converges around the outside table.

"To Letitia," Natalie says, raising her glass, as she always does at these get-togethers. They clink glasses.

Later, getting ready to leave, Natalie is taking her empty Tupperware back to the car. Though Upeksha had protested, Natalie had bought the steaks, marinated them, and brought along her favorite salads.

She's changing their dance, just a little bit.

Grant is taking things out of his ute. He stops and stares at her, his lip curling in distaste.

"Fucking wogs," he mutters under his breath.

He still can't get his racist slurs right.

He looks like he's about to say something else, but then Griffin appears with more Tupperware. Loaded up with leftovers this time.

"Your mum insisted," he says. Natalie rolls her eyes.

She glances back toward Grant, curious, but he ducks his

head down, pretending to look for something in the ute. *More of the same*, Natalie thinks to herself.

To her surprise, it doesn't affect her the way it usually does.

Griffin shuts their boot, and takes Natalie's hand.

He kisses her gently on the lips.

Then they walk together inside, to say their goodbyes.

GOOD GIRL BAD - EXCERPT

S.A. MCEWEN

A perfect life, or a perfect lie?

Rebecca Giovanni has a beautiful life—a job she loves, a new husband who's a great deal better than the old one, and two charming daughters from her first marriage.

It's hard not to be smug about how well she's done for herself.

She trusts her new husband.

Then she wakes to find him and her sixteen-year-old daughter missing. Their dog is dead, and the front door is wide open.

No matter what the police insinuate, Rebecca cannot believe Leroy and Tabby went anywhere together willingly. She's doing a stellar job, but blended families always have their difficulties. And they'd never leave the house without their phones and wallets.

But where are they? What happened in the house that night?

Rebecca's younger daughter is acting strangely, and her ex-husband is hiding secrets of his own—like where he was that night, and the real reason that he left Rebecca.

And Rebecca can't help thinking about the last time she saw

her husband, and heard him say something she'd rather forget...

Monday

The house is silent.

Eerily so.

Rebecca Giovanni stands at the top of the small stairway to the kitchen. Below her, her sixteen-year-old daughter Tabitha's miniature poodle, Charlie, lies on his side. He could nearly be sleeping, except he never sleeps in the kitchen, on the cold tiles. Rebecca can see that something is wrong, the position of his legs not quite right, his little head stretched back at an unusual angle, a rigidity about him sufficient information such that Rebecca does not go any closer; does not check.

Beyond him, the front door is wide open. A cold wind blows in from the street, through the leaves of the wisteria hanging lushly around the veranda, caressing Rebecca's forearms, swirling beyond her into the silent house.

The faint scent—her favorite flower—drifts past her toward the very back of the house, where her youngest daughter Genevieve is still sleeping. At fourteen, she is well and truly a teen when it comes to sleeping in. The house could fall apart around her and she would not so much as mumble a complaint. Rather, she'd roll over, tugging the doona around her ears, eyes resolutely shut against the intrusion.

It's spring—November—but still cold, and Rebecca shivers.

Leroy was not in their bed, and Tabitha was not in hers, either.

Rebecca's eyes roam around the kitchen.

She is not worried yet.

She notices Leroy's phone and wallet next to the fruit bowl; he has not gone far.

Tabby's phone, usually glued to her hand, is hanging

precariously over the edge of the dining table. It looks like it should be falling, not balancing there.

But other than that, the house looks much the same as it always does when Rebecca gets up.

Rebecca is still not worried, despite the open front door, and despite the dead dog in her kitchen.

She's not worried yet.

But she will be.

Chapter 2

Six Months Earlier

Rebecca smooths her Armani skirt across her thighs, a tiny, self-contained movement that she uses as a break in conversation. It makes her look calm and certain; it soothes her when she needs to take a moment to think of what it is she wants to say.

It also reminds her of who she is: successful. Capable. In charge. The mother who wears Armani to parent-teacher interviews, her makeup flawless, all poise and perfection.

Rebecca doesn't speak rashly. She weighs her words, her cool blue eyes resting on the recipient appraisingly. In this case, the recipient is Tabitha's home room teacher, Ms. Paisley.

"I'm not sure what you're getting at?" she says eventually, her gaze unflinching.

Ms. Paisley is young. Much younger than Rebecca, with kind brown eyes, which are right now blinking too frequently.

Nerves? Rebecca wonders.

She is used to people being nervous around her. Being wowed by her, in fact.

"Well, it's my first year teaching Tabby, of course," Ms. Paisley responds, her words tumbling over each other in her haste to get them out. *It's probably your first year teaching, period,* Rebecca thinks to herself, patronizing, but she keeps herself in check. "So I've only known her for a few months, obviously. It's just, she's always been one of our top students, and certainly her work earlier in the year was of a consistently high quality. It's just the last month or so that things have started to slip a little. Work not handed in, or not much effort applied, that kind of thing." She nearly looks apologetic, but seems to be trying her best not to. Even as Rebecca watches, she pulls her shoulders back and sits up a little higher in her chair.

"I'll have a word with her. But she's been her usual self at home. I haven't noticed any changes." Here Rebecca stops. *Typical,* she thinks. Just as she was taking ownership—"I" haven't noticed any changes—she spots Nate fighting his way around chairs and parents to reach them. Rebecca watches him silently. It's characteristic of her ex-husband to be late, and to look the opposite of calm and poised. Rebecca wonders if people think less of her because she was once married to him; if she's tainted by association.

"Sorry I'm late," he puffs as he comes to a halt beside them, casting about for a spare chair he can pull up. Spying one halfway across the room, he disappears again. Rebecca turns back to Ms. Paisley, who looks as though she's very happy to wait for Nate to return.

Does no one have a sense of time and urgency except me? Rebecca thinks. If the roles were reversed, she would plough ahead without the late ex-husband. She would say what needed to be said to whomever was present, and conclude the meeting decisively, precisely on time. Too bad, so sad if you were late and missed half of it.

She runs her hand over her skirt again, the soft black fabric feeling expensive and luxurious under her touch. It clings to her thighs elegantly, ever so slightly suggestively, the muscle underneath nicely defined by regular weight classes and running. She raises her eyes to Nate again, her expression patient to anyone who didn't know her well.

To Nate, the patience is feigned, or mocking.

Here we are, waiting for you, again.

He seems unfazed though. He plonks the chair down next to Rebecca, and beams at Ms. Paisley.

"How's my girl doing?" he says, and Rebecca has to stop herself from rolling her eyes.

"We're well past that, Nate," she says, cutting Ms. Paisley off, and summarizing the meeting so far, her demeanor crisp and business-like. She doesn't give Nate a chance to respond, but addresses Ms. Paisley again with the air of someone who is used to making all the decisions.

"So, I'll have a word with her. I'm sure it's nothing to worry about. Tabby has always been a hard worker. If necessary, I can always limit her phone time. That's always rather motivating for her."

Ms. Paisley looks surprised, and starts to open her mouth, but Rebecca cuts her off. "Did you have any questions, Nate?"

"Yes, actually," he says, though he knows full well that the question was rhetorical, designed to show Ms. Paisley that they were co-parenting cooperatively. Rebecca didn't really expect him to say yes—to the point that she was half rising from her chair, and stops mid-air.

She glances at Nate, something hard passing across her face fleetingly, then she smiles and sits back down. Poised and gracious.

"Well, obviously we'll talk to her," Nate goes on, glancing at Rebecca. "But have you noticed anything at school that might explain it? Any change in her friendship group? Any boys she's hanging out with, that might be breaking her heart?" Nate looks like he is joking, making light of it, but Rebecca can see that he's just not sure how appropriate it is to ask Tabby's home room teacher about her love life, so he's disguising it under a protective, jovial father spiel.

Joke, joke, joke.

Rebecca thinks Nate is wasting his time. *Her* time.

Of course Tabby isn't seeing anyone.

Rebecca actively discourages relationships—she thinks Tabby is far too young, and has more important things to do. Like excel at school and get into a good university. The truth is, though, that Rebecca would have no idea if Tabby was romantically involved with anyone; they don't have that kind of relationship. Her certainty is rooted entirely in confidence that Tabby would not defy her wishes. She's not worried by Ms. Paisley's revelations. Tabby is strong-willed, and can be a little bit feisty, but she falls back into line when Rebecca flexes her parental rights.

For the briefest of moments, that reality is held up for her to examine, and the starkness of it feels uncomfortable, and nags at her. *Should she know her daughter better? Should her certainty be rooted in dialogue, not authority?* But she turns her thoughts back to the issue at hand.

"I very much doubt Tabby's been distracted by a boy," she says, somewhat pompously, and Ms. Paisley looks apologetic again.

"Well, actually, there has been a lot more socializing between the boys and girls this year, and I have noticed Tabby spending a lot of time with a particular young man, Trent Witherall. Has she mentioned him to you at all?"

Rebecca's demeanor shifts slightly, her posture stiffening, her jaw tensing. Nate glances at her uneasily.

"No, nothing," Rebecca says, her voice tight. She looks to Nate for confirmation, this time appearing genuinely interested in his response.

"She has mentioned Trent to me, yes," he says, directing his words to Ms. Paisley. "But she's never made it sound like they're dating, or that she likes him in particular. His name has just come up a few times when she's talking about her friends, what they're doing on the weekend. Do you think they're...seeing each other?" Nate is aware of something simmering in Rebecca next to him, and he keeps his eyes carefully on Ms. Paisley.

She, likewise, speaks back directly to Nate. "I would have thought so, yes," she says, but won't be drawn into why she thinks that. "I really think that's a conversation for you to have with your daughter, don't you think?" she hedges, and Nate wonders what she has seen.

Hand-holding?

Kissing?

Do kids kiss on school grounds these days? He can't even remember how you wooed girls back in his day. He can't imagine his broody eldest daughter being buffeted about by the strong feelings of young love.

But broodiness would be the perfect breeding ground for that intensity, that all-or-nothing consuming infatuation, wouldn't it?

Nate suddenly feels old and out of touch. Unlike Rebecca, he *has* noticed a change in his daughter. He would have said it had been much longer than this year though, and doubts very much it has anything to do with Trent Witherall. In fact, if his life depended on putting a date to it, he would have said it was a year or two ago that she started to become more withdrawn, more secretive. More broody.

About the time that Rebecca married that twerp, Leroy, in fact.

He steals a glance at his ex-wife. She is sitting very still, projecting that calm, reasonable, I-am-listening-to-you-deeply facade. He wonders if Ms. Paisley can see through it.

He wonders what sort of man *can't* see through it.

What sort of man would fall for it.

He did, sure. But he was so young.

You can't put an old head on young shoulders, his father used to tell him, and he understands the saying differently now.

But Leroy is his age. Forty-five, give or take a few years.

What was Leroy's excuse?

Or was he just as stupid as twenty-year-old Nate?

And if Leroy was just as stupid as a twenty-year-old, what might

have gone on between him and Nate's sweet sixteen-year-old daughter,
that might explain the changes in her mood?

Back at home, Rebecca dumps her handbag on the kitchen island with a loud thump.

She can hear chatter coming from the living room, the faint hum of the television, and she feels like storming up there and shutting it down, all of it. The television, the happy family time. Tabby has made her look stupid in front of her teacher, in front of Nate, but she's just glibly fooling around on a school night in front of the television without a care in the world.

"Tabby!" she shouts down the hallway, and there's a moment's silence, the voices quieting. Then the living room door opens and Leroy and Tabby both emerge, padding down the long hallway toward her. They look so easy, so relaxed, and she feels resentful that she has to be the one to bring things back to order, to interrupt their fun, to remind them of the real world.

But somebody has to do it.

But just as she opens her mouth to say something cross, something biting, Leroy jumps clownishly down the five steps into the kitchen and grabs her in a dance pose, swinging her around, one arm firmly around her waist. He grins at her impishly.

"Look out, Tabby, Becci looks a bit peeved! What is it? An F? An expulsion? You've learned that Tabby's quit math to do embroidery instead, and your dream of retiring on the back of your daughter's orthodontic practice has gone up in flames?"

He spins her around once more and then pushes her against the wall, kissing her right on the lips in front of Tabby, his eyes laughing.

They'll have sex tonight, she can tell from his kiss, the way he holds her against the wall.

Her tummy flutters.

"Slipping grades," she squeaks, as she tries to wriggle out of his grasp, but the tension has gone out of her.

Leroy gives her a final smooch, then releases her. As he turns to go back to the living room, to give her space to chat with Tabby, no doubt, she thinks she catches a small smile toward her daughter, and a wink, and her stomach does less of a flutter and more of a churn.

Chapter 3

Monday

Rebecca shakes Genevieve roughly.

"Gen. Gen!" Genevieve groans, and tries to burrow back under her doona, but Rebecca is tugging it down harder and faster than she can pull it back up.

"Mom!" Gen protests, the cold creeping in from the hallway, from outside. From the situation in the kitchen.

"Where's your sister?" Rebecca's voice is urgent.

"Wha-at?" Genevieve rubs her bleary eyes. "How should I know?"

It's now nearly 9 a.m. Two hours have passed since Rebecca found the front door open, and impatience and irritation have finally given way to something more urgent.

"Get up," Rebecca instructs her youngest daughter, rifling in her cupboard and throwing a tee shirt and some leggings at her. Genevieve holds them up in confusion. They're not appropriate for a Melbourne spring morning, no matter that it's nearly summer. And they're certainly not appropriate for a school day.

"They're gone," Rebecca continues, looking through Genevieve's wardrobe like she might find some clue in there. "Leroy. Tabby. Leroy's car. But something's not right. I can feel it."

Hustling Genevieve through the house, shivering in the thin tee shirt Rebecca had handed her, she points to the mobile phones and wallets triumphantly. "See? Tabby would never go anywhere without her phone. And. Charlie." Here she glances at the little form underneath the sweater she had hastily thrown over him while she made phone calls, trying to find her daughter and husband.

Her eyes linger there, uneasily.

In her state of agitation, she completely forgets how one ought to break such news to anyone, especially to her teenage daughter.

Genevieve is still half asleep, and is struggling to make sense of her mother's words, which are being thrown at her, staccato-like. Bam. Bam. Bam. Bam. But when her eyes—following Rebecca's—fall on the shape under the sweater, she falls silently to her knees. She glances up at Rebecca, a question in her eyes, but she doesn't need a response, and her mouth gapes slightly, tears welling in her eyes, and she doubles over, a silent scream emanating from her open mouth.

She doesn't touch the sweater, just keens silently beside the little body on the floor.

Something about her daughter's grief shakes Rebecca out of her quest for an explanation. Genevieve is a thoughtful, sensitive, quiet teen, and Rebecca is surprised by the force of her pain.

No, that's not right. She's not surprised by the force of it—she's surprised that Genevieve is showing it. To her mother.

Rebecca has her own pain about the dog, but it's been swallowed up by more important things, like where her husband and other daughter are, and why they left in such a hurry that they didn't even shut the front door.

She kneels beside Gen, putting her arms around her shuddering, small frame. "I'm sorry, I'm sorry," she whispers, mortified by her insensitivity. She holds Gen tight, keeping her close until her shaking slows and stills.

"What happened to him?" Gen hiccups, her voice painfully small.

"I don't know, sweetheart. But something's wrong. I'm going to call the police. I've already called everyone who I can think of who might know where they are."

She'd been methodical—Tabby's friends. Trent Witherall's parents. Nate. The school.

Miss Ambrosia, the cafe where Tabby works on Saturdays— only to be told that Tabby hadn't worked there for over four months.

Where was Tabby going on Saturdays, then?

Where was she getting money from?

Rebecca mentally kicks herself. She'd looked into GPS tracking when she'd bought Tabitha her first smartphone. For a while, she'd obsessively checked her location, but Tabby was always exactly where she said she'd be. Even after that interview with Ms. Paisley, when Rebecca was watching her closely, checking her location again daily—well, she'd gotten slack. She thought Ms. Paisley had it wrong. Tabby was never over in Richmond, where Trent lived. She was always with her best friend Freddy, studying, or else at work.

Rebecca had stopped checking. She really didn't think Tabby was the type to sneak around.

Now, though, she wonders what data she'd be able to access. Tabby's phone was right here. Didn't Google Maps keep data on everywhere you'd been? Was that true? And if it was, please dear God let Tabby's passcode be the same as it always was—the day she got Charlie, her twelfth birthday present. But he had arrived a week early, so it wasn't like she was using her *actual* birthdate, which Rebecca had told her a hundred times would be foolish, anyone could guess it.

Now, she grabs the phone off the table, presses the home button. Nothing. The phone is dead, and she scours around for a charger, usually lurking in every second power point, so many phones seemed to populate their home.

Personal phones. Work phones. Kids' phones.

Old, discarded phones.

Finally, she spies a cord hanging out from under the microwave, and plugs Tabby's phone in. It takes forever even for the little red battery symbol to blink on. Impatiently, she turns away from it.

"Did you know Tabby had quit Miss Ambrosia?" she asks Genevieve, trying to be gentle, but it's hard to keep the urgency, the accusing tone out of her voice.

The girl has pulled Charlie's stiff little body onto her lap. So different from Tabby, Genevieve is short and dark-haired, her brown eyes now staring vacantly into the distance. Charlie was Tabby's dog, but Tabby shared him generously with her little sister. She made sure to give Genevieve turns walking and feeding him, so the dog loved them both eagerly, joyously. Right above her, in fact, is an enlarged photo of the three of them. Charlie is clutched between the two girls, the love on their faces palpable through the camera lens. Tabby is crouched down— she's easily a foot taller than Gen. Her long, blonde hair is sun-bleached and messy, cascading over a slim, tan shoulder. Her blue eyes sparkle, staring right at you out from the wall.

Rebecca shivers. Leroy loves that picture. "Bottled joy" he called it, insisting that it was the one they frame, but it's always made Rebecca uneasy. Tabby looks older than she ought to in it. In a tank top and tiny shorts, she looks worldly, seductive. When she'd snapped at Leroy that perhaps that was why he liked it, he'd looked at her strangely. She still can't quite fathom the look that he gave her.

"They look like happy kids," he'd said, and she wondered if he could sense her jealousy, if that was why he was so restrained. God, she was basically accusing him of lusting after her teenage daughter, he was well within his rights to fly completely off the handle. Instead, that strange look. Like he didn't even know who she was in that moment.

It wasn't as simple as the ageing mother envying the blossoming of youthful beauty. Rebecca herself was beautiful, she had no doubt and no insecurity about that. Tabby even looked a lot like her, really. Taller and slimmer, but their features were similar, their striking blue eyes.

No, it wasn't that. But it was hard to put her finger on the pang that the picture gave her, every time.

She wished she'd put her foot down, ordered a different print.

Now, though, she focuses back on Genevieve, who solemnly shakes her head.

Rebecca has no reason to doubt her. Gen has always been compliant, cautious, responsible. Tabby is more like her, Rebecca —impulsive, flamboyant. Sure of herself.

Or at least, she used to be.

Is she still flamboyant?

Things have changed, Rebecca knows that. But they've changed so slowly, so incrementally, that she hasn't paid that much attention. Now, though, she realizes that the word *flamboyant* no longer applies to her eldest daughter.

Genevieve, on the other hand, was never flamboyant. Genevieve is steady. Calm. Rebecca trusts her absolutely.

Rebecca casts her mind back to the Saturday just gone. Tabby had left on her bike at about 11 a.m. as she always did. She covered the lunch shift, making coffees and toasting fancy baguettes for a little café one suburb over from them. Or at least, that was what she was supposed to be doing. Rebecca was sure, in fact, that Tabby had boasted of a promotion not that long ago. Managing that shift. Definitely not more than four months ago.

So where had she been going every Saturday for four hours?

"Did you call Freddy?" Gen's voice is faint. Rebecca thinks that she hasn't grasped the seriousness of the situation. All she can think about is the damn dog. And the dog definitely needs thinking about, but right now, Rebecca just wants to know where Leroy and Tabitha are.

"Yes. I spoke to Fred. They haven't seen her this weekend. Freddy had already left for school by the time I called."

Fred and Frederica. For the hundredth time, Rebecca thinks *how vain. Silly*, even. To choose a name for your kid that's basically the same as your own. The amount of times there's been confusion over who is being referred to when you say "Freddy" is ridiculous.

Tabby and Freddy have been best friends since grade four, and Fred, the father, has promised he'll get Freddy to call Rebecca when she gets home from school, in case she knows anything. The way he says it makes Rebecca's stomach churn again.

In case she knows anything.

But Rebecca shoves that feeling aside and calls the police.

Chapter 4

Monday

By the time Nate arrives, the police have already been at Rebecca's house for an hour.

A bored-looking officer stops him at the door, asking for identification and a reason for being there.

"My daughter is bloody missing with *that man!*" He has to stop himself from shouting the last two words, his voice rising unusually high.

Rebecca looks over at him, disdain written all across her face. Even disdainful, she's still a striking woman, with her aquiline nose and astonishing blue eyes. She's fitter than when they were together, too—always shapely, she's now toned as well, and her posture is that of a lioness, queen of her terrain.

The officer's ears prick up at Nate's tone, though. "We don't have any reason to suspect anything suspicious at this stage, sir," he says. "But can you tell me why you refer to Mr. Giovanni in that manner?"

Nate can't though. He's never gotten along with Leroy, but do you usually get along with your replacement in the husband department? Leroy is too smooth, too handsome, and Nate is sure he'd be a player. The thought of him living with his teenage daughters is a constant thorn in his side. When Leroy had first moved in, he'd had to be very firm with Rebecca about some boundaries.

Leroy can't shower the girls.

He can't be in the bathroom with them.

At the time, they'd been ten and twelve, and Rebecca had just nodded and smiled sarcastically at him, but he could see how close she was to rolling her eyes. Because of course the girls didn't need any help in the shower, and of course even Rebecca would have thought it weird if her new boyfriend had wanted to spend time in the bathroom with her tween daughters. Rebecca was clearly humoring him. But she didn't know men the way that he, Nate, knew men. Tabitha was a knockout. Even at twelve, men did double takes on the street. She looked like she was a model, with those long, lean, tanned legs and waist-length beach-blonde hair. She didn't look away, either. She'd fix those smoldering eyes on whoever stared, her face deadpan, neither shy nor embarrassed nor egotistical.

He often wondered what went on behind her eyes, but he never asked.

She was going to break hearts, though, and Nate would be damned if he'd let a grown man spend any time with her naked.

Now, though, he's forced to backtrack. Because what could he say?

The man would have to be blind to not ogle her, to not notice her in a sexual manner?

No. He was being ridiculous. He knew that. He was just paranoid. You hear so many awful things these days. It was a terrible time to have a daughter.

To be a woman, he corrects himself. *It was a terrible time to be a woman. Or had it always been a terrible time, and now they were just starting to shout about it?* #MeToo had shaken him. And then there was the "incident" on Messenger. Here he cringes slightly, the

police officer watching him curiously. It was all too difficult to
think about, and he's whittled it down to a simple concept, one
which was, however, impossible to enforce: *he did not want men
thinking about his daughter in a sexual manner at all.*

Ever.

For the rest of her life.

Did all fathers feel like this? It was a constant mild panic, a
sense of tension he could never quite shake. How dangerous the
world might be for someone so beautiful.

Now, he wishes he'd asked what Tabby was thinking behind
that blank expression when men stared at her. At the time, it was
too uncomfortable. Embarrassing, even. What do you say to your
daughter about men his age staring at her on the street? He
always felt mortified, as though he was part of that group, like he
needed to collectively apologize, like he was tainted by their
stares, too. Like she might think less of him because weren't they
all just a little bit like him? On the surface, at any rate. He
couldn't quite put his finger on it. But it was awful and
uncomfortable and he pretended it wasn't happening at all.

Now, he wishes he had some idea what her views were on
middle-aged men. He wishes he'd been more proactive in talking
to her. Guiding her.

Protecting her.

He shakes his head at the police officer. "Nothing, sorry," he
says. "I don't trust my ex's new husband, that's all."

"But it's just a gut feeling, isn't that right, Nate?" Rebecca
interjects, her voice jeering at him ever so slightly. Nate ignores
her.

"Is there any news?"

"Well, no one has been able to locate Mr. Giovanni or
Tabitha, but given there was no sign of forced entry, and Mr.
Giovanni's car is gone, it does suggest that he and Tabitha have
gone somewhere together. We do understand that Mrs. Giovanni
feels that that is extremely unlikely, but at this stage, I'd suggest

waiting until tomorrow to see if this all sorts itself out. These things usually do. Alternatively, if you want to file a missing person's report, we need you to come down to the station." The officer snaps his notebook closed with an air of finality, nodding to his colleague, a silent agreement that it was time for them to go.

"What about the dog?" Rebecca asks, her voice high. She has one arm wrapped around Gen, and Nate moves forward to give his youngest daughter a hug. He strokes her hair and pulls her head onto his chest, murmuring gentle words to her. Gen starts crying quietly again, but Nate can't tell if she's worried about Tabby or if she's crying for Charlie.

"Yes, the dog is concerning." The officer consults his notebook, as though that will help him clarify what has happened here, what the solution might be. But he doesn't add anything else, and Nate grits his teeth.

"What happened last night?" Nate turns to Rebecca, his voice tight. "Did you have a fight? With Tabby? With Leroy? How was she yesterday? Did she seem okay?"

Rebecca's face closes. "She was fine. Wasn't she, Gen? Except..." Here she glances at the officers uneasily. "Apparently she quit her job months ago. But she's been pretending to go every Saturday like usual. Did you know that?" Her tone is accusatory, as though Nate being privy to something she wasn't privy to was the worst thing about that piece of information. She sounds defensive, *and so she should be*, thinks Nate. Saturday is Rebecca's day to look after the kids. *What else was she not keeping track of?*

Nate shakes his head slowly. "So where was she going?" he asks, his eyes conveying the challenge he would never dare to say aloud: *Why weren't you looking after her properly? Why weren't you paying more attention?*

But the police officer interrupts them. "We'll be off now. But do keep in touch and get back to us if they haven't turned up by tomorrow." He goes to hand Nate a card but Rebecca snatches it out of his hand, her eyes flashing. "Great," she snaps. "Just great. I'm telling you that things were tense between them."

This is news to Nate, and he looks up sharply.

"I am one hundred percent sure they wouldn't go off sightseeing together. And leave their phones and wallets behind. Something is wrong, and isn't it your job to find out what?"

"Whoa, whoa, back up a minute," Nate interjects, nodding to the officers who are heading for the door, despite Rebecca's wrath. He assumes she has discussed this tension with them and their assessment of the situation still stands, so he says, "Thank you, officers. We'll be in touch." Then he turns back to Rebecca. "What's this tension between Leroy and Tab? How long has it been like that? Did something happen?" He knows his suspicions are written all over his face, that Rebecca can see through him, can even probably anticipate the self-satisfied "I told you so" on the tip of his tongue, but he doesn't *want* it to be true. He wouldn't mind being right for once, in this particular relationship, but not about this. Despite his eager jumping on this news, he really does just want to find Tabby and check she's okay.

That she's not fooling around with Leroy, who even Nate has to admit is shockingly good-looking.

Sexy. Alluring.

"It's nothing." Rebecca stares back at him coldly. "He's just been really on board with parenting her, and she resists it, you know? Says he's not her dad. Yada yada yada. Exactly what you'd expect from a sixteen-year-old toward her stepfather setting boundaries."

Nate studies his ex-wife carefully. There's something she's not telling him, but he can't guess what it is. *Is it a subtle dig, that he's not pulling his weight in the parenting department? That Leroy has had to take up the slack?*

"Where is Leroy on Saturdays when Tabby does her

vanishing act?" he shoots back, and for a moment he sees a flash of doubt on Rebecca's face. She composes herself instantly though, looking at him pityingly. "My husband is not looking for any extracurricular entertainment, Nathan," she says archly. "We are extremely happy. If you want to know so much about what our daughter gets up to, perhaps you should do a little more with her yourself." And Nate winces, because it's true, he used to have the girls more, he used to have Tabby on Saturdays in fact, but things had come up, life had gotten in the way, and Tabby wasn't even home on Saturdays anyway, so what did it matter if they were at Rebecca's house just one extra day a week? He still had them two days a week, and for most of the holidays.

His thoughts are interrupted though, by a small sob from Genevieve, and Nate realizes with a guilty start that he had forgotten she was even there, listening, and maybe Rebecca was right, maybe he *was* a shit dad.

Who would focus on making accusations rather than comforting their daughter?

"Hey, hey," he says, his face softening, and he reaches for Gen again, pulling her small, compact little frame into his arms. "Let's think about a funeral for Charlie, hey? We'll have it when Tabby's back. But we could make some plans, now. Maybe choose a tree to plant?" Nate's mind is working overtime. He's never been a fan of dogs, but he knows Genevieve is going to need a lot of support over this.

And also, he wouldn't mind taking her out of Rebecca's house and asking a few more questions about what she saw last night.

Not least because he might have been parked outside her house for a good portion of it.

Visit www.samcewen.com to find your preferred store.

NOTE FROM THE AUTHOR

I'm acutely aware of the danger of cultural appropriation in trying to tell a story like this. For those wondering, yes, I consulted with someone with Sri Lankan heritage for this book, though this book is more about a broader refugee experience than about Tamil or Sinhalese people or their history and struggles.

Likewise, I consulted with a working escort for this book. Natalie offers only one very privileged perspective of sex work. Sex workers are as variable as workers in any profession. Some hate their job, some love it, some can pick and choose their clientele, and some need to take any work to survive. You probably know a sex worker or two, without knowing their profession. They're people, just like everybody else. So be an ally. Vote for decriminalisation. Dehumanizing sex workers is a slippery slope for human rights.

Finally, I feel acutely how lucky I am to have been born in Australia. And it is just that—luck. Refugees are you and me, with worse luck. We can never know the choices we would make under the circumstances that they face.

I love Glennon Doyle's phrase "there is no such thing as other people's children." Alan Kurdi, and every other child refugee, were and are our children, just unlucky enough to be born somewhere not safe for them to stay. It is beyond devastating to me that we are not protecting them.

I wanted to write a story to honour that.

A note about sex work

Please also note that 'sex worker' is the preferred title. The word *prostitute* is dehumanizing and thus can be dangerous for sex workers. It is used in this novel in certain contexts as the killer is dehumanizing his victims, and it is likely the term that he would use.

It is also offensive to refer to a sex worker as a whore. Workers may refer to themselves in this manner, but people outside the work cannot without causing offense.

This novel portrays the work of only one way of working in the sex industry. It is that of a very privileged worker who is able to pick and choose her clientele, and avoid some of the more dangerous and dehumanizing aspects of the work. It is in no way intended to represent all sex workers, in particular workers of color. Though I have hinted at the impact of race on sex workers, that is a whole other topic beyond the scope of this book.

ACKNOWLEDGMENTS

To Stephanie—thank you. I am in awe of you every day. I am so proud and feel so lucky to call you my friend.

To Sarah—thank you. Your wise words, your sharp wit, your amazing insight and your willingness to read my half-baked drafts have made this book so much better. I'm so sorry I keep failing to deliver you the romance I keep promising.

To Justin—thank you. Your feedback meant so much to me. Really, really, a lot. You have no idea. Even if I left in the dodgy romance lines ;)

Thank you to The Tension Dilemma - http://thetensiondilemma.com/ for the use of some content. For anyone wanting more insight into how to be a better ally to women of colour, read this blog.

To E—for the insights about sex work. Thank you.

To Catherine Deveny—thank you for taking the time to read my draft, meet me to chat and provide such a thoughtful overview. You helped me to see the bigger picture and gave me the courage to not try to fit this story into a box. And, of course, thanks again for Gunnas (and the omelette mix), a truly fabulous class.

Victoria Colotta—thank you for your thoroughness, your thoughtfulness and your honesty.

To Erica Russikoff from Erica's Editing Services—thank you once again for your exceptional editing and your thoughtful feedback and care with my book.

To Elizabeth Mackey for my beautiful cover—thank you.

And to all of you reading this book—thank you for taking interest in it. I really appreciate it, and I hope that you enjoyed it. x

ABOUT THE AUTHOR

S.A. McEwen writes nuanced and gritty psychological/domestic thrillers exploring relationships, especially within families...with a particular interest in how the dark gets in, and the complex things that drive us toward or keep us out of connection with each other

She is a qualified social worker and works as a clinician and educator in youth mental health, and lives in Melbourne, Australia with two gorgeous boys and a puppy.

If you've enjoyed her writing, please get in touch and say hello! The links are listed below.

Get notified when I **release a new book** via my newsletter here: www.samcewen.com.

f facebook.com/authorsamcewen

a amazon.com/author/samcewen

BB bookbub.com/authors/s-a-mcewen

g goodreads.com/samcewen